Rejected By The Alpha

Juana Makan

Ukiyoto Publishing

All global publishing rights are held by

Ukiyoto Publishing

Published in 2021

Content Copyright © **Juana Makan**

ISBN 9789364946339

*All rights reserved.
No part of this publication may be reproduced, transmitted, or stored in a retrieval system, in any form by any means, electronic, mechanical, photocopying, recording or otherwise, without the prior permission of the publisher.*

The moral rights of the author have been asserted.

This is a work of fiction. Names, characters, businesses, places, events, locales, and incidents are either the products of the author's imagination or used in a fictitious manner. Any resemblance to actual persons, living or dead, or actual events is purely coincidental.

This book is sold subject to the condition that it shall not by way of trade or otherwise, be lent, resold, hired out or otherwise circulated, without the publisher's prior consent, in any form of binding or cover other than that in which it is published.

www.ukiyoto.com

Dedication

To Miss Rachel who painstakingly sending emails for the betterment of this book.

To Ukiyoto Publishing, a big thanks for allowing writers and readers to meet through you.

To Catherine, for being a fan, a critique, and a believer.

To unnamed individuals that helped in any way.

Above all, to God Almighty that made all possible.

Acknowledgement

I would like to express my gratitude to Miss Cherry for the message she sent not so long ago that jumpstarts my writing prowess as well as Stary Writing for giving amateur writers an opportunity to bring out fiction stories in the online world.

CONTENTS

The Sweetest Goodbye   1

The Comeback	5
On A Friday Night	6
The Real Boss	10
You Know What To Do	15
Threatened	19
Will You Or Will You Not?	20
Liaison With The Boss	24
You Look Like Someone I Knew	29
Mira's Secret Service	31
The Welcoming Committee	35
When The Spark Is Gone	40
Nostalgia	45
Show-Off	51
Under Dog	56
Remnant Of The Past	61
Morning After	66
Lucy's Day Out	111
Calm Before The Storm	115

The Sweetest Goodbye

Remus found Becca at the hill. The teenager was under an old tree. He smiled when he remembered their conversation not long ago. The teenage girl believed that she owned the old tree. She considered the tree hers since they were the only pack members that spent most of their time at the hill. However, between the of both them, Becca spent most of her time after training under the old tree. If he was mistaken, the tree was planted by his great grandfather. Needless to say, it was at This same hill that he and Becca started training together years ago. He found her doing exercises meant for training warriors. Instead of mocking the thirteen-year-old girl, he taught her some moves he had learnt during the training

Becca had earned his respect the first time he caught her in the hills. The teenager knew what she wanted in life. It was quite obvious that she adored her father, the current gamma of the pack. She wanted to be a warrior just like him. Unlike most girls her age, she started working on what she wanted to be. Becca did not mind getting herself dirty or sweaty. She did not even blush at his presence, the incoming alpha. With a sigh, he approached the gamma's first born.

He sat beside the fifteen-year old girl. Becca remained focused looking at the cabins below the hills. The training was usually done at this time of the day. The sun already low on the horizon. It made the view below even more mesmerizing. The dim light from the sun added a panoramic view to the territory. The hills were also part of the territory of Cloudless Moon Pack. The pack also owns various acres land across the deep forest. Due to the wide expanse of the territory, the members of the pack to run freely in their wolf forms away from the prying eyes of the human population. At the center of this huge land and is a business area. Remus and his pack were werewolf shifters. Currently, Luke Franklin, Remus' father holds the position of the alpha. Soon, he will be made alpha. The alpha title has been in Franklin's family for generations. The previous alphas of the Cloudless Moon pack thought ahead. They built amenities that would be convenient to the pack. One part of the packhouse was the office of the alpha, luna and beta. They shared a conference room designed for a maximum of 20 participants while the other part holds the cafeteria and the infirmary. Another building in the pack has four floors. It accommodates the pack's school, from pre-school to middle school. The members of the pack didn't attend human school until they reached senior high or wanted a degree.

There was also a park, an ice cream and pizza parlor nearby. A coffee shop and two bakery shops were beside the convenience store. These businesses are owned by the pack members. They rent it from the alpha but the money goes to the pack's coffers to pay for the convenience of every members of the pack. The alpha wanted the pack to be self-sufficient. The services rendered by every member earned a decent salary for them to provide for their family and themselves. The alpha's family also has other investments outside the pack territory. Needless to say it, most of the pack expenses were catered for.

"When are you leaving?" Becca broke the silence, bringing him back to the present.

He and his father had conversation couple of days ago. Though he no longer needed convincing since he knew that he had to undergo the same training his father had gone through as an heir to the alpha position, the knowledge that he had to leave for a long time made him sad. It would be a long time, months or maybe years, before he would be back to the pack. His father already instilled in his young mind the obligations of a future alpha and the things that he had to you be fine there?"go through and the possible sacrifices along the way. He turned to the girl beside him. She still refused to glance at him.

"Tomorrow at dawn." He responded.

Guilt marred his face when he heard her sigh. They had gotten closer due to the training they had together. The training they went through improved their skills. It also helped him somehow. He never knew he had the patience to teach someone, anyone. Well, Becca was a fast learner. He sent her a sad smile when their eyes met. He felt bad when she did not reciprocate it.

"Why didn't you tell me? I had to hear it from my parents."

"Because I thought it would hurt less. I'm sorry, Becca."

"Will you be fine there?"

"Of course, buddy. Father won't send me there if his only heir would be in trouble.The hint of sadness eased from his heart when he heard her chuckle and finally faced him. The gloomy expression in her face eased a little.

The atmosphere lighter compared to a while ago.

Her laughter could light up the place. Remus noticed this from their years of friendship. Whenever he heard her giggle or smirk, he knew that the rest of the day would be a lot better for him.

"I'm gonna miss you, alpha."

"I'm gonna miss you, too, loser."

"Hey!"

The girl tackled him to the ground. Before he could defend himself, Becca sat on his middle and he was pushed onto his back. It never fails to get the girl agitated hearing the word 'loser'.

A mad Becca is way cuter than a calm Becca.

"Take it back!" She screamed.

Laughter echoed in the hills as they bickered and fought for dominance. Sadness was lost in the wind.

It was going to be a while before they had this moment again. Maybe not, since alpha responsibilities were awaiting Remus.

For sure, everything will certainly different when he comes back from his schooling abroad. But, the pack comes first.

The Comeback

Full and satisfied, Becca made her way to the hill. It was few minutes walk but it would be worth it. The trees protect her from the blazing heat of the sun.

The hills always gave her a sense of peace. The stillness of the place calms her. She even visited the hill on the first day she came home from semester break.

Summer still had a month before it turns into another season. Another season meant another semester for Becca. She would have shorter nights and more books to read. However, she knew that in the end it would pay off but in the end she wanted to become a warrior like her dad, her parents allowed her to get a degree in college. Only then will she be allowed to do whatever she wanted.

Enjoying the wind slapping her face, she stopped on her tracks when she saw a guy standing under her tree. She did not have a clear view of the guy's face but his stance held familiarity.

Becca felt a sudden sense of possessiveness. Who dared to stand and touch her tree? Yes, she owned that tree. She considered it hers since she has been the one to find the tree. Her heart beat accelerated as she neared. The wind blew stronger and the strong scent of lemon with a hint of freshly cut wood hit her. She sniffed harder. Her eyes glued to the guy on the tree, the guy under her tree turned towards her.

"Mate." They both whispered.

6
On A Friday Night

Tapping the counter with her left hand. Becca motioned the bartender for a refill and the guy immediately obeyed. "One for me, too."

After gulping down her drink she asked for another one before glancing at the person who sat beside her. Janessa nodded at her before swallowing her own drink. The bartender did wait to be told. He refilled both their glasses.

"Fancy seeing you here, boss." Becca mumbled.

"I would say the same with you."

They made a toast with their glasses before drinking together.

Janessa Doue is her boss in the perfume company she was currently employed at called La Belle Scents where she works as an account manager. She has been working with the company after she graduated college six years ago.

Janessa is younger than Becca by a couple of years. However, Janessa is smarter than she looks. Becca had witnessed it with her own eyes. It was a sight to behold when Janessa countered the ideas of the other managers during previous meetings. Her fresh ideas brought big money. They have worked together many times in the past. Janessa handled the marketing department in the company. She works as the marketing director. The woman was simply a genius. The sales shot up like an atomic bomb a few months after the young woman had taken over the position in the company.

"Nice tatts, by the way."

"Thanks, boss."

They both glanced at her left arm. Printed in her skin was an image of a wolf with blue eyes. It also had a crescent shape of the moon facing upward.

"The eyes are familiar though." Janessa piped in.

"Really?"

Janessa nodded then turned to the bartender.

"Bills on me."

Before Becca could protest, Janessa already handed her card to the bartender. The younger woman shrugged.

"Thanks."

Becca replied.

"Enjoy the rest of the night."

Having said that, Janessa sashayed her way out of the now packed bar. Several pairs of eyes followed her as she marched toward the exit.

"She's a piece of art." The bartender suddenly said.

"And a woman of substance." Becca added before looking at the bartender.

"Is she yours?" He asks as he wipes the counter.

She shook her head.

"She's my boss."

"From your eight o'clock." The bartender uttered as he poured her another drink. Becca had her fill and nodded before leaving.

She made her way towards the exit Janessa had used.

The cool air greeted her face the moment she opened the door. She pulled her jacket closer to her body. She was almost nearing her car when someone called for her attention. She glanced back but did not bother stopping.

"Aren't you going to thank me for the drink?"

Becca stopped by her car and opened it before turning to the woman. She was wearing a knee length dress with a leather jacket covering her upper body.

"Thanks for the drink." Then gave her a smile before sliding the driver's seat.

She left the bar in slow pace. Having a drink by herself in a crowded bar was a usual scene for Becca. However, when someone tried hitting on her, it's a sign for her to leave. She neither went to the bar to look for bed warmer nor company. She goes there to calm herself.

"I'm sorry you have to be by yourself."

Becca smiled when she heard that from her head. It was her wolf, Lucy.

Every werewolf shifter shared a wolf in their head. Their life would be easier if the person and the wolf were in good relation. There were cases were humans and their wolves were always in conflict. The human would be considered a rabid wolf that has to be put down or the wolf would never be let out again."

She responds sadly to her wolf.

"It's okay. Someday we'll have someone who would accept us and won't allow us to be gloomy all our lives."

"I hope so, we'll have our second chance Becca. Goddess Selene knows we deserve it."

"Thanks, Lucy." She replied hopefully. The drive back to her apartment was in comfortable silence after their conversation. Becca started working in La Belle Scents after she moved into her apartment. She resided on the third floor of the five-floor apartment building.

Life has been good to her since she left the Cloudless Moon Pack. The support from her parents did not stop after she was 'almost' banished from the territory eight years ago. It was not an easy start being alone in the human world. Her family supported her at since she left.To make the summer holidays bearable, she applied for part time jobs. She also seeked the permission of the nearby pack, who was an ally to the

Cloudless Moon pack, to use their land if she wanted to let Lucy out. The only time her family was complete was when she graduated in college. Being with them was a priceless gift.

The latin honors she received from the university could not be compared to the presence of her family.

"Home."

Becca chuckled when Lucy purred as she closed the door to her unit. She tossed the keys into the wooden bowl on top of her coffee table.

"Can I have a bath? My fur felt lifeless already."

'Yes, ma'am."

Becca was lucky to own a big bathroom in her apartment so that she could be in her wolf form and stll have little more space to roam around.

If there is one thing that she and her wolf loved doing , it was bath time. Being a neat one, Lucy likes her soft and fluffy. On weekends, Becca made sure that Lucy could indulge herself in the shower.

"Did you buy that shampoo that I saw on TV?"

"Yes, ma'am." Becca replied then proceeded to fill the tub with water and scented oil that Lucy loved together with the dog shampoo that Lucy asked about.

When the water was cool enough, she covered it with bubbles, Becca could almost imagine her wolf jumping up and down in her head. She stripped then placed her clothes in the hamper to make room so that Lucy could have enough space when she turned into a big wolf. Without wasting time, Lucy immediately sank into the tub while Becca let her wolf enjoy herself. She settled peacefully at the back of her mind.

10
The Real Boss

Becca picked the printed copy of the report that Janessa had asked for this morning. It was the sales report of the last three months.

She placed the papers in a folder and left her office to Janessa's office which is in the next floor.She used the fire exit to get there. Ruth, Janessa's secretary motioned her to go in directly. She nodded at the secretary then knocked before pushing the glass door open.

"Please put them on the table." Janessa ordered without looking at her. Her focus was on her computer screen.

"Everything alright?" She opted to ask since the young boss seemed on edge.

"N-no. I mean, yes." The young woman spoke up. A few tendrils of hair falling from her bun. The stress did not even let Janessa eat her lunch. Becca knew she was strained because of the many years they had worked together. She could not count the times Janessa. Often, the woman was still calm even under pressure.

"Anything I can help you with?" Becca asked.

Janessa sighed and sat up straight.

"The big boss is coming today."

"Oh? It's why everyone is on edge."

"You're not one of them?". Janessa queried.

Becca nodded her head. "I'm doing my job well. I have nothing to worry about." Janessa pouted. "I wish I feel the same."

"Relax. The company has been doing great. We're selling big time in the market under your management." Becca said. She and Janessa have been in a great relationship professionally. They became friends when

Becca was promoted to being the account manager. They worked together most of the time and their friendship blossomed along the way. Becca worked under Janessa. She handled the major accounts in the company. The other account officers seek her opinion instead of going to Janessa directly. That meant less workload for the marketing director.

She and Janessa organized meetings together. They brainstormed before and after every conference. Most of the time, they were the last to leave the office.

"Boss, Madamme Doue will be here in 30 minutes."

Ruth announced.

"Thank you, Ruth."

Janessa said then proceeded to take deeper breaths. Becca motioned on the young woman that she was taking her leave. When Becca arrived in her own office, she grabbed a spare flash drive from the drawer. She opened several folders and started working on the files. Ten minutes later, she saved everything in the flash drive. She grabbed the tiny storage then she stood up. She made her way to the next floor. Ruth was not at her desk but the door to the marketing director's office was ajar. She knocked before opening the door. Janessa was quite irritated when she glanced at Becca. Ruth was seated there too. She lifted the hand that holds the flash drive. Janessa's left eyebrow raised.

"The sales of last year in bar form. I also have the graph of the sales last five years. The sale of every perfume from January until last month."

The young boss approached and collected the flash drive.

"Get your laptop, Becca. See you in the conference room in 10 minutes."

"What?"

"Tik-tok."

She saw Ruth grinned widely before they left the office.

***

The moment Becca opened the door to the conference room, she froze. There were two women but her eyes remained the woman speaking to Janessa. Their similarities were noticeable. They were both petite and slim though Janessa looked an inch taller. They both have platinum blond hair. Though different in color, the expression and shape of their eyes were the same. Their conversation halted as they turned to her. Becca's brown eyes met blue. The exact same color of the eyes of the wolf tattooed in her arm.

"About time you arrived." She heard Janessa say.

"I thought this is just the us." The other woman said.

"She made a more concise report. Can you believe that she made the report 15 minutes?"

Janessa praised.

"Maybe I should promote her and fire you."

"No, Aunt Mira. You need my genius brain in running this company."

"Smart ass."

"I am."

The woman named Mira looked at Becca before settling in one chair. "Tell me what I need to know." The older woman replied.

Janessa motioned for her to move to the front.

"Please."

She opened her laptop and connected it to the overhead projector. She then inserted the flash drive and she opened the folder inside the memory storage.

"If you're ready."

Becca handed over the presentation to Janessa and relaxed. Since Becca already knew the content of the presentation, she focused her attention on the older woman. For years that she had worked in the company this is her first time seeing the owner of the company. There were no pictures on the internet about the person behind the La Belle Scents but only a very short information regarding the owner. The big boss as Janessa had said a while ago, is obviously older than both of them. She should be in her early to mid-thirties. She has pale skin and long, straight hair that reached her mid-back. From a short distance, Becca noticed the dust of freckles on top of the woman's pointed nose. There were a few more on both her cheeks.

"What do you say, Aunt Mira?" Janessa inquired.

"Impressive."

"Thank you."

"You have the position until I say so."

"Yes, boss." Janessa said with a wide smile. She followed it with a salute.

"By the way, this is our account manager, Becca Jackman. Becca, meet the elusive woman behind La Belle Scents, Mirabella Doue." Becca stood up immediately and held her right hand out to the big boss.

"It's a pleasure, Miss Doue."

The woman stood up, too, and met her eyes. They had a stare down. Becca was about to put her hands down when Mira took it with hers. Sparks exploded inside her.

Becca took a deep breath and smiled at the big boss. A smile that was never returned.

"Treat your boss to lunch, Janessa." The older woman said but their eyes were still on each other.

"Yes, ma'am. You should come with us, Becca."

Janessa offered.

"I don't want to intrude, boss. But thank you."

She then excused herself from the conference room. She could still feel Mira's eyes behind her back. And her system still buzzing with sparks since their hands shook.

Juana Makan

You Know What To Do

Holding her wallet in one hand, Becca grasps the mobile phone in the other. She steps back as more people enters the elevator. Conversation about work ensue. It is currently time for lunch and most of the employees were on their way out of the office. Almost half of the employees eat at the cafeteria located in second floor.

Becca was having a conversation with a fellow employee when she felt eyes on her. She glanced around as her colleague continue speaking. Two tables from hers sat the big boss. Her arms were crossed in front of her. The older woman looked away when their eyes met. Distaste painted in her face though.

Becca noticed that no one seemed to notice the big boss of the company. No one recognized her. Perks of not posting her picture in her biography. Mirabella Doue attained privacy at its finest.

"That's Miss Doue, right?"

"What?"

Becca turned her attention to the woman she shared the table with. Her name is Angela. The woman offered her table when she was looking for a seat a while ago.

Miss Doue was waiting in line. She found Janessa at the cashiers desk. She was already paying for their food. Her eyes followed the younger boss as she sat on the same table with the big boss.

"Is that her sister?"

"Maybe."

Becca finished her drink and excused herself from Angela. She threw the trash into the garbage and dropped the tray on top of the others beside the garbage bin. She made her way to the elevator and pressed the floor number of her office. It three days since she first Miss Mirabella Doue. The moon goddess has blessed her with a second mate. This time a woman. Remus was her first mate. She and Remus learnt about it when they met again at the hill eight years ago.

She was surprised knowing that her childhood friend and alpha was her mate. Clearly, the knowledge came as a surprise to him too. However, what came next was an even bigger surprise.

The sound of the door opening stopped her from going down the memory lane. With a heavy heart, she alighted from the elevator and made her way into the safe confinement of her own office. The first thing that Becca noticed when she reached her table was the yellow post-it on top of the laptop.

Meet me at the conference room after lunch. - M

Lucy is literally doing happy dance in her head.

When Becca recognized Mira as her second chance mate, Lucy's joy knew no bounds. Her wolf was very happy that the goddess had them a second shot at happiness.

It was mind blowing that the second mate the goddess had gave them is a woman.

Lucy fell in love at first sight when she saw Mira in the conference room. Her wolf did not question the choice of the moon goddess regarding their second mate.

It came as a surprise for Becca that her wolf immediately accepted their second mate. Knowing Lucy as vain and half the time a proud primadonna, it was indeed a startling behavior for her wolf to quickly accept the gender of their new mate.

If not for the reign of Becca over her wolf, Lucy would have shown herself to their mate the first time they met.

"Go and freshin' up. Our mate is waiting."

"Can you be calm, Lucy?'

"Oh, please. I've been waiting for this to happen."

"What do you mean?'

"Mira is our second chance at happiness. Don't let her go this time, human."

"Why are you so accepting, Lucy? Why aren't you questioning that our mate is a woman?"

"Duh. You're the only one who's in denial, Becca."

She could imagine her wolf rolling her eyes at her before retreating to the back of her mind. She followed the advice of her wolf. She went to the washroom and quickly checked her appearance. She brushed back her bob styled hair with her fingers. She tried to remove the creases of powder she had applied on the blue long sleeved polo shirt that she is wearing. She folded the sleeves a few inches from the wrist. It showed the snout of a wolf inked in her skin. As the employees returned to their respective offices, Becca used the fire exit to reach the floor above. No one was in the hallway since the floor only houses two private offices, a conference room and a showroom. Becca did not bother knocking. She pushed the glass door open and made her way inside. She noticed the big boss comfortably sitting in a chair. Her blue eyes were on Becca's the moment she stepped inside.

"Good afternoon, Ms. Doue."

The blonde haired woman nodded at her before motioning her to sit on the chair in front of her.

"Do you know who I am?"

That was the first statement she received the moment she sat down. Becca glanced at her boss before shaking her head.

"Aside from being my boss, I don't know anything about you."

"From what pack do you belong, Miss Jackman?"

She stared at the woman in shock. She was answered with a reprimanded look similar to a teacher guarding detention.

Becca cleared her throat to compose herself then takes a deep sigh.

"I was part of the Cloudless Moon Pack." She responds after a while.

"How's Luke?"

Puzzled, Becca leaned on her chair and fixed her eyes on her.

"I know of the existence of the werewolves. I'm not as naive as my niece. Besides, not everything you see is what it seems."

Becca nods in agreement. "Why am I here?"

"I just want to know if you're a liability to my company."

"What's the verdict?"

"We'll see."

Becca takes in a deep breath before standing up. Like always, Mira's eyes were following her movement.

"I should go. Work is waiting."

She moved towards the door.

"One more thing, Ms. Jackman." She stopped when she reached the door. "You know what to do if you don't want that woman to lose her job."

She did not respond. She left the conference room. Lucy however is currently doing a happy dance like a man on cocaine.

Threatened

"Let her know that, Jackman. Or else, she'll have her last paycheck by the end of the month."

Scratching the nape of her neck, Becca nodded before following her boss out of the coffee shop.

Becca couldn't help but wonders how old her mate is. She acts like a teenager.

Will You Or Will You Not?

"I was afraid. I still am." Becca admitted.

"Why? Is it because I'm a woman?"

Becca shook her head. "You're my second mate."

"W-what?"

Mira sat up. Her long, straight hair cascading down her back.

They faced each other.

Becca smiled sadly at her mate. Mira was still frowning at her. She sighed as she gripped the blanket tighter.

"I got rejected by my first mate. I was twenty."

Sympathy crossed Mira's face. The next thing she knew, the petite woman is already on her lap. Her pale arms around her shoulders.

Having second thoughts, her hands remained under the blanket. She basked at the unexpected affection she got from the Mira..

"Hug me back, goddammit !"

Chuckling, she put her arms around Mira. She could not help but sniff the sweet scent the woman emitted. It is a mixture of honeysuckle and a hint of freshly brewed coffee.

"It feels great, right?" Mira whispered into her ear. Bringing cold shivers down her spine.

"Yes. It feels really great."

She pulled her mate closer. Mira did not protest. They stayed like that for a while. Lucy stayed surprisingly quite too.

Mira let her go then looked down at Becca with a smile painted in her lips.

"One man's loss is another man's gain."

"You believe that?"

"Yes, Ms. Jackman."

"One thing though," Becca uttered. "I'm not a lesbian."

One brow raised, "Are you sure about that?" Mira visible on her beautiful face.

Becca could hear Lucy laughing in her head. This is the first time her wolf made her presence known since she woke up. However, Lucy let her know that she was having a time of her life having her mate in her arms.

"I never had a girlfriend before." She disclosed.

"Good. Neither do I. Let this be a first and the last."

Becca was engulfed in a hug once again. This time, she tightened her arms around her mate. She did not wait for Mira to demand it from her.

"I've waited for you for so long." Mira whispered.

"You do? How long?"

"Decades."

"How many?"

"About eight or so."

She smiled then caressed Mira's back. "How old are you?"

The petite woman pushed her back a little then smiled at her before pinching both her cheeks. "I'm friends with Luke's parents."

Becca laughed out loud hearing that. Her mate frowned at her.

"How old are you exactly?" She asked again.

"A hundred and twenty."

Becca's eyes widened then hastily proceeded to check for wrinkles and lines on her mate's face.

"What are you?"

"I'm a witch. Janessa's mother is my younger sister."

"But Janessa's mom looks older."

"Because my sister indulged her human mate. The guy wanted them to grow old together." Mira explained and rolled her eyes at the end of the statement.

"How old is your sister?"

"Eighty-three. My mother met her mate after she got me. She got pregnant with me when she was still a young witch in late 1800s."

Becca stared at her mate, flabbergasted then suddenly blinked when Mira pressed Becca's forehead with her index finger.

"You'll watch me die then?" Becca asked.

The witch glared at her mate. "Of course not. I'm going to make a potion that will make you live longer. Besides, werewolves have a longer lifespan than a regular human."

Becca nodded in agreement. Her hand stayed on Mira's waist as they stared at each other.

"So, you're going to accept this bond?" Mira asked.

She had this hopeful look in her eyes. Becca stared at the older woman with tenderness. Might as well allow herself to enjoy the luxury of having a mate.

"If you'll have me." Becca replied.

"Of course, silly."

Becca giggled. She caressed her mate's smooth face with her finger and sighed in content.

"My wolf is having a party in my head. She's very happy."

"The feeling is mutual. Unfortunately for her, her human is a slow poke." Mira teased with a wide smile in her face.

"Hey, this woman is inexperienced and young." She did not fail to stress on the last word.

Her mouth went ajar when she received a small but hard pinch on her side. This small woman sure do possess long nails!

"Respect this old woman, young one."

This time, it was Becca who glowered at Mira. However, the other woman sent her a bright smile that melted her irritation.

"Kiss me, old woman."

"I thought you'd never ask."

They smiled as their lips met. Becca pulled the petite woman closer as Mira held onto the taller woman's shoulders as their kiss deepened. Finally, this is what it felt like to kiss a mate.

Liaison With The Boss

A sudden embrace brought Becca's attention back to her surroundings. Upon seeing the pair of pale arms around her waist and the sparks it brought, she immediately recognized that it was her mate.

She was currently working on the sales report sent by account officers from different malls of the State that sold their product.

Later on, she would be coordinating with another account supervisor from the three States under her jurisdiction.

Smiling, she glanced at the woman who now held her full attention. Mira smiled back before kissing her cheek. "Good afternoon, babe."

"It's afternoon already?"

With a knowing look, the petite woman glanced at the opened data in the monitor.

"Busy day?"

"A little."

Becca moved the chair to accommodate her mate. Mira leaned her butt on the table and faced her.

"It's past noon. Now I know why I didn't see you at the cafeteria." Becca took a quick look at her wrist watch. The time states that it was already two in the afternoon.

"I got caught up with work."

Mira did not say a word instead grabs Becca's left arm and pushed the sleeve of the light green dress shirt Becca wore. She folded the ends until it almost reached her elbow. Becca watched her mate as she did that. The petite woman traced the tattoo on her with her finger.

"When did you get this?"

"Five years ago."

"It's the exact color of my eyes."

"I noticed."

Grinning, Mira met her eyes. "I like it. Is this your wolf?"

"Yes."

"When will I meet Lucy?"

"Soon."

She already told Mira about her wolf. Lucy was ecstatic when their mate asked about her. While Becca was explaining to her mate, Lucy was leaping for joy in her head that she had to stop for a bit. She needed to calm Lucy so that she and Mira could talk without interruption.

Becca peeked at her mate through her lashes when Mira caressed her face. She tried to suppress her smile when she found Mira staring at her lips. Their eyes met before Mira moved her face towards her.

Her brow raised when Mira's face appeared only a few inches away from hers. She chuckled when her mate pouted. Becca placed her hands on each side of the petite woman's hips before pulling her into her lap.

Mira circled her hand on the taller woman's nape when their lips collided. Becca released a moan when her mate starts playing with the hair.. She quivers in pleasure.

She squeezed the skin on Mira's neck before pulling back. Mira's eyes were closed and her lips slightly swollen as a result of their heated kiss. Becca dropped a peck on those inviting lips.

Lust pooled at her mate's eyes when she opened her blues eyes. Becca smirked. She felt somewhat egotistical knowing that she had brought those emotions to this well composed woman.

She received a glare from Mira when she saw the smirk on her face. Mira moved and settled comfortably on her lap. However, the red tint on the older woman's cheek did not escape the sight of her mate.

Mira pressed her heated cheeks against Becca's neck. She received a pinch from her mate and she was not able to stop the giggle that escaped her lips. She drops a kiss on Mira's forehead.

Their moment ended when they heard a 'ping' sound from the laptop. It indicates that new emails just came in.

Mira released a sigh. "Play time's over."

"Some people have to work to live." Becca answered playfully.

"Work kept you from me."

Becca dropped another kiss on her mate's lips when the petite woman pouted. "Should I resign and make you my sugar mama?"

"No. You need to work for the both of us. My money's on Janessa's trust fund."

"Oh? Poor me. Should I go to the bigger fish?" Becca retaliates as she strokes her mate's back who is contentedly leaning on her front.

Emails keep on coming. Those were from the account officers around the State. Those mails maybe the reports she asked for during the meeting via zoom.

"Don't even think about it. I'm going to curse them all, wolfie."

"Wolfie? Very original."

Instead of striking back, Mira bit her shoulder. Becca made a soundless cry when she felt teeth piercing her skin despite the shirt she has on.

"How old are you again?"

"Two."

"More like two hundred."

She pulled away when the petite woman tried to grab her hand to have another bite. Becca seized Mira's hand instead.

"Can we just kiss, babe? I'll be black and blue if you keep on doing what you're doing."

Mira grinned like a Cheshire cat when her hands were released. The look on her face promised naughty thoughts.

The older woman grabbed her mate's face. She smiled before their lips met especially when the petite woman bit Becca's lower lip.

Apparently, Becca is the battered mate between the two of them.

After a few minutes of kissing, Mira stopped attacking her lips.

"I'll get you food. People may think you have a wicked boss."

Becca's eyes followed Mira as the petite woman straightened her dress. Another kiss later, her mate left her office.

Like a newly charged battery, she faced the emails with vigor.

She was on the phone when Mira returned carrying a brown bag. Becca could perceive the greasy goodness the moment her mate entered the office.

Mira laid the food on the table then put aside the documents on Becca's table to make room for the food.

Becca smiled when she caught Mira sneaking some fries into her mouth. Before she could protest, her mate put one in her mouth, too.

The working woman chewed it immediately before answering the queries of the person on the other line.

"Send me the files before 6PM today. Thank you." She said and ended the call.

The smell of the cheeseburger assaulted her nose. It made her stomach churn.

Mira pulled an extra chair beside her.

Becca smiled at her mate and mouthed "thank you."

"I could get used to this." She uttered.

"Not a problem, babe. Dig in."

She pressed a kiss on Mira's temple before grabbing the burger. She did not know she was starving until she smelled the greasy goodness.

Having a caring mate ain't bad after all.

She sent a thankful smile towards Mira.

You Look Like Someone I Knew

"**D**ad sent me here to tell you about the situation in the pack."

"I understand."

Becca pushed her plate away. She had suddenly lost her appetite knowing that her family is in danger.

"Dad has been very thorough with the training schedules. The security has been upped."

Becca nodded. She sighs with worry.

She feared for her family. It was quite worrisome knowing that these attacks could kill people in the pack. She might have been gone for a long time but Cloudless Moon Pack would always be a home for her. "I remember!"

The Jackman siblings turned to Mira when she unexpectedly speaks out. The petite woman smiled sheepishly. She even blushed with embarrassment.

"You have a cunning resemblance with Seth."

"You're acquainted with Dad?" They said together.

Mira nodded. Becca felt her squeeze her hand again.

"How?"

"He and Luke were friends when they were still kids. They were a dynamic duo. They pranked any member of the pack."

"W-what?" Confusion marred Jake's handsome face.

"Long story, baby boy. I'll tell you later."

"You and Seth are like twins in different era."

"I've been told so."

Mira beamed at the young man. Confusion was still plastered on Seth's face.

Mira's Secret Service

Becca was currently working on the files of a major account when Janessa barged into her office. She noticed her immediate boss looking around her small space. The younger woman did this like it was the first time she had been in her office..

"Yes, boss?"

She stared at Janessa before returning her full attention back to the reports sent by the account officers. The report should be in prints by the end of the week.

When five minutes passed, she was yet to hear anything from the young boss. Becca stopped what she was doing then leaned on her chair and watched Janessa as she scrutinized the interior of the office.

Her office looks like any other regular office. The space is small but works just fine for Becca since she does not entertain visitors often.

There was a table, a swivel chair and one other chair in front of the table for any possible visitors but often, it was Mira who used it.

There was also a set of drawers on one side. Documents piled up in thick folders there. Those were also printed reports of the previous years.

The marketing director touched the dried flower on the table and frowned suspiciously.

Mira had put it there the day after they finally accepted the bond. She did not protest since it added character to her impersonalized working table. The flowers also gave off a sweet scent that relaxed her mood as she works.

"What are you to my aunt?"

Becca leaned They were having a stare off but Becca remained collected.

"This is heather. Do you know what this flower can do?"

Becca glanced at the dried flowers again. Several small flowers grew in the body of the stemmed plant.

Mira collected a number of stems. She dried them and put them in a wooden vase. It was very simple but elegant. It added elegance to the otherwise very plain table.

"I don't know. Miss Doue put them there. She said that my table looks livable with the flowers on it."

"The flowers protect the person beside it from black spells." Janessa said in a very serious note. "We have that in our home in several places. I even have them in my bag."

Astounded, Becca stared at the innocent flower.. She grinned at her mate's simple but not very obvious way of showing concern.

"You know what we are, right?"

Becca nodded.

She heard Janessa sniff. The young woman's frown deepened.

"What's wrong?"

To her surprise, Janessa was sniffing the heather. Becca found herself again under the scrutiny of the young boss. The young woman crossed her arms in front of her.

"That scent. Do you have any idea what that scent can do?"

Becca shook her head. "No but it calms me."

One brow raised, Janessa voiced out. "That old brat is marking you, Becca."

"What do you mean?" She asked, trying to hide the smirk on her face. She was loving the gestures her mate was showing her.. Her intentions were on point but very subtle.

"Aunt Mira has been around since the both of you met. She considered herself retired the moment I stepped foot in this company." Janessa disclosed. "That changed when she saw you in the conference room.

She suddenly has an interest to be around but her ass can't even stay in my office for more than twenty minutes."

Becca laughed out loud at her young boss' outburst. She received a glare for her action.

If Janessa were to be in a children's cartoon show, she might be portraying a character that has fire blowing in her nose and ears as she talks in annoyance. Becca knew that the irritation that the young woman felt was not towards her but to her aunt who is currently not present.

They could talk now since it was only the both of them. As she mentioned before, she and Janessa were friends but in the presence of other employees, Janessa still has the last word.

"What's with you and that old witch?"

Becca chuckled. Her friend was going straight to the point.

"Mira and I, we are together." She admitted.

She did not see the point of hiding it anymore. She had been avoiding her mate before. This time, she could say it out in the open. Mira and her accepted the bond already, anyway. Besides, her mate did not deserve to be hidden. Anyone would be proud of that old witch."

"Together? You mean, you and Aunt Mira are dating?"

She nodded. "I'm dating your Aunt, boss." She said with conviction.

Janessa giggled. "I knew it!"

Becca smiled at her friend. If there was one thing that Janessa and Mira have in common, they were a little bipolar. However, Janessa seems genuinely happy for them.

"It's now absolutely clear that you're indeed playing for the other team."

"What?. Becca uttered in surprise.

The young woman glanced at her, one brow raised. "You never look at men. Not even a single peek. Women flock at your side."

"What?"

"Becca, if you only notice the way the employees in this company look not that they really care about those rising sales you pull off, you should be aware that most of the women here desire you."

"What?"

"I perfectly understand why Aunt Mira sprayed that scent in your office."

"W-what?"

"Something is wrong with your vocabulary, woman."

"What?"

Janessa takes a deep breath, gave Becca a quick glance before walking out of the office. The young woman waved as she left.

Becca's eyes turned to the dried flowers when she was left alone. She sniffed. The scent was a little sweet. It just tickles her nose buds but never irritates the olfactory sense. In fact, the scent was very relaxing. She remained leaning on her chair but her eyes were glued on the dried heather. She grinned widely. Becca noticed that sometimes the sweet scent sticks to her clothes. Since it wasn't too strong, it did not bother her. Whenever the scent sticks to her clothes, she notices that no one seems to approach her like most of the time. In case someone did approaches her, the interaction would last for not more than five minutes. She chuckled. The sound reverberated in the small confinement.

Mira knew how to shoo the competition away. And she did it in a not very obvious manner. A sneaky witch. Literally. With a great change of mood but a happy one, she sniffed again before going back to the sales report that awaited her expertise.

The Welcoming Committee

The sun was barely up when Becca started her trip. She rode the first flight home. It was a journey eight years overdue. She rolled down the window of the car she was driving to her destination. She had a car rented from the nearest facility immediately she arrived the airport. She already called a few before her flight. Becca placed her elbow on top of the open window then glanced at the green vegetation along the way. She missed having the wind kiss her face while on a road trip. She smiled as she inhaled the fresh air.

She ate the free breakfast from the plane. It was a poor substitute for the hearty breakfast she always had but it would do for the next two hour. She forgot to stop at a drive-thru due to the excitement to be home.

Becca slowed down when she approached the border of the pack territory. From her peripheral vision, she could see the faint shadow of a werewolf imprinted on the lines of the trees beside the long road towards the center of the pack land. The werewolf has been following her car the moment she entered the Cloudless Moon pack terrain. Truth be told, Becca is waiting for the warriors to stop her car in the middle of the road. However, she reached the center of the town but no one stopped her.

People eyed the unidentified car. Wariness showed in their faces. Some people hid their children behind them.

Becca perfectly understood the parents' action.

Expansions have been made on the buildings in the commercial area of the territory. Eight years have completely changed the atmosphere in the children's park. Many more equipment were added in the play area. There were additional food stalls, too.

Becca stopped by the pack house then parked her car in the nearest empty lot.

She took a deep breath before she getting down from her car. She held her mobile phone in one hand while the other held her car keys.

"Becca?"

She turned to the familiar voice that had called her. Her smile widened when she saw the surprised look on her father's eyes. Seth Jackman approached his eldest child. He gathered her in his arms. Becca hugged her father back. She pressed her face into her father's chest. She grinned when she heard her father sniffing her hair. He always did that. She and her mother always tease him a lot about it. It may sound creepy but it is his way of assuring himself that his mate and pups were indeed around and safe.

"I'm okay, dad."

"I know. My baby girl is here. Please allow your old man to hold his daughter."

Becca couldn't help but laugh at her father's emotional action. She tightened her arms around him. Seth let his daughter go slowly. His eyes were a little misty as he stared at his first child. He blinked twice. Becca was still with him, and beside him in the pack territory. What he saw seeing was not a fruit of his imagination. His first child was indeed here with him. His wolf howled in his head in confirmation, too.

"Where is mom?"

Becca asked.

"In the infirmary. Your brother is in the training room. They have a session for a hand to hand combat until noon."

"You're not handling it?"

"I was but I received a report that there was an incoming unmarked car heading to the pack house."

She beamed at him.

"I'm sorry about that." Her dad smirked at her before messing her short hair. "You're a welcome distraction, baby girl."

With an arm crossed along her shoulder, Seth led his daughter towards the infirmary.

Her mother was in the clinic when they found her. Like what her mate did, Olive approached her daughter and gathered her first born in her arms.

A lone tear fell from Becca's eyes as she hugged her mother. She missed her. Both of them. A lot.

"I'm happy you're finally here. I missed you Becky."

"I missed you too , mom."

She said then kissed her mother's cheek. Olive gave her daughter a wide smile.

"I'm sorry, baby. I'm supposed visit you–'

"I understand." She cut whatever her mother was about to say..

"How long are you going to stay?"

Her dad asked.

"I'm not sure, dad."

"I know this is hard for you. Adding the circumstances, it's not the best time."

"I'll be fine. You raised a strong daughter, Seth Jackman." She beamed at her parents. Hopefully it gave them assurance that she was in fact alright.

"Let's have lunch. I know you're starving." Seth said, changing the conversation.

"I'm famished." Becca yelled out.

The three of them marched toward the cafeteria. There were a few people who were already having lunch. There were three people waiting in line for their turn.

Becca and her mother look for a table while her dad ordered for them.

"How are you, mom?"

She started when they found a place to sit.

Olive smiled sadly to her daughter.

"It's bad. Many members of the pack turned up injured in at border. Security has been upped but we're still on alert."

She held her mother's hand in hers.

"It's not a good time for you to be here, Becca."

She didn't get to respond because her father arrived with the food.

Behind him was another guy with a tray full of food.

If her eyes can turned into a heart shape , this is probably the right. Food could make her bad day go away. It was a mood changer.

They thanked the guy as he placed the tray of food at the table.

"Your brother will be here any minute now. I didn't tell him that you're here."Seth said, smiling widely.

"He would be very surprised."

Her mother added.

"It has been a while since we've eaten together." Her dad chipped in

A cheerful smile plastered on Becca's lips. Seth kissed his mate's temple while Becca squeezed her mother's hand in assurance

"Will you be staying with us?" Her mother asked.

"I was thinking of barging into Jake's cabin."

"It's a bad idea. Your brother's place is not meant for a human dwelling."

Becca and her dad burst out laughing with her mother's immediate response. Jake have always been the messy one in the family.

When Jake turned eighteen, their parents gifted him a cabin of his own because they knew that sooner or later he would eventually find his mate. In Jake's terms , he simply needed his own space.

However, even though he has his own place, Jake still comes to eat in his parents' house most of the time. His alibi? He does not have time to cook for himself since he is busy with the warrior training. Smart guy.

When The Spark Is Gone

Praying for more courage, Becca made her way to the alpha's office.

She and Jake were not able to see each other at lunch since her brother was caught up with pack stuff. However, it was a great opportunity for her and her folks to catch up.

It is currently two o'clock in the afternoon according to her wrist watch.. She had learnt from her dad that the alpha was always in his office around 1PM.

Taking another deep breath, Becca knocked on the wooden door. Since the office is sound proof, she turned the knob after a warning knock.

The current alpha raised his head when she entered. He had documents on top of the table.

Becca noticed that he was not surprised seeing her. They stared at each other for a couple of seconds before he nodded in greeting.

"Come in."

She closed the door and approach the table. He signed a couple of pages before closing the folder then put it aside.

"Good afternoon, Alpha." Becca greeted.

"Hello, Becca."

He responded then stood up and extended his hand for a hand shake. She stared at his outreached hand before clasping it with hers..

"I would like to ask for permission to stay for a few days, Alpha Remus." She disclosed with a regained confidence.

He tucked his hands into the pockets of his trouser. He did not sit back. Rather, he stepped toward the glass windows. It overlooked the training field.

"This is not a good time, Becca." Alpha Remus disclosed. His face showing little to no emotions but it was quite obvious that the current situation in the pack meant great deal to him.

"My father told me about it." Becca responded.

He nodded.

"How long are you going to stay?"

"Three days, Alpha. No more than a week."

He nodded again.

"Please follow the protocol."

She nodded, too.

"Welcome back, Becca."

"Thank you, Alpha Remus."

She bowed her head in respect before leaving the office.

Upon closing the door, a wide grin painted her lips. She pressed her right knuckle against her chest. It was beating pretty normal. She had never been this thankful feeling her heart thump normally.

A fake cough took her out of her reverie.

Her face heated up when she found an unfamiliar woman standing a couple of meters away from her. The beautiful woman her age smiled at her startled face.

"Did the alpha do something to you?" She asked in a very friendly manner.

Becca shook her head.

"He actually allowed me to stay for a few days." She responded with a smile.

"That's nice. I'm Luna Felicia."

With a wider smile, Becca bowed her head in acknowledgment.

"Hello, Luna. My name is Becca Jackman. I'm the daughter of Gamma Seth and Olive Jackman."

"Nice to meet you, Becca. Your mom told me about you. She misses you a lot."

The luna is slightly shorter than her by a few inches. Her welcoming smile is the most striking feature about her face. Becca stepped aside to avoid further obstructing the door to the alpha's office.

"Enjoy your stay, Becca." The Luna said before walking away.

"Thank you, Luna."

Becca bowed before walking away.

Her steps felt lighter. Her heart felt better, too. So much better. Lucy was wagging her shaggy tail. She was also grinning in her head. Her tongue on the side of her big mouth, wagging as well. Becca traced the road back to the rented car she parked in front of the pack house. The drive to her parents' house did not even last for five minutes. Her father's truck was parked in the garage. She parked hers by the side of the rough road. With the duffel bag in hand, she marched toward the cabin that housed a lot of her childhood memories. Knowing that her parents hid a spare key under the small pot beside the window, she unearthed the slim gold metal and pushed into the keyhole. She laughed out loud when she found Jake in the living room. He was munching on a cold pizza as he watched television. Her only sibling almost fell on the floor when he saw her. Half of the pizza slice hanging on his mouth. He immediately stood up and pulled her in his arms. He gripped both her forearms when he let her go.

"You're here."

Jake mumbled.

"Yes. You are, too." Becca replied.

He chuckled.

"Folks always have food."

She removed his greasy fingers from her body then moves to occupy the chair he had vacated.

"Your room is clean. Mom cleans it at least once every week. You knew where the sheets are."

"Thanks."

"Now I knew why Dad mind linked me to have dinner here later. I thought they missed my awesome self." He ends it with a wink.

"Where's the mushroom?" Jake asked.

Becca snickered. Mira and her brother had developed an awkward liking to each other.

"You missed her?"

He shook his head.

"I'm fine without her in the same space."

"Because your heart can't take my awesome self."

The pizza in his hands flew from his hands including the one in his mouth. Becca noticed that Jake jumped at least one foot in the air. Her brother also released an ear-splitting sound upon seeing Mira beside him.

Becca looked down. No matter how much she wanted to toned down her voice her laughter echoed in the house.

"Bitch, get out!" Jake screamed, his eyes wide with terror.

Her beautiful mate grinned at him before walking towards her. Becca reached for her hand and pulled the petite woman until Mira sat on her lap.

The tall woman noticed that she liked having Mira on her lap. She loved hugging the petite woman from the back. She felt so much better having her mate in her arms.

"I missed you, babe."

Becca muttered.

"I missed you, too."

Mira replied dropping a kiss on Becca's lips before encircling her slim arms around the tall woman's neck.

"The romance is choking me. " Jake reacted. His voice a normal tone.

"Did the parents know that you brought this mushroom here?"

"No, Later at dinner." Becca replied.

"Are you going to stay at your parents, babe?" Mira asked

"Yes."

"Can I stay with you?" Mira pleaded.

"Of course."

"I'm going to puke." Jake uttered when Mira gave her a peck again. To agitate him more, Mira grab both her cheeks and kiss her lips repeatedly. She made sure that it made a sound in every peck.

"See you at dinner."

They both chuckled when he left. Mira stayed on her lap though. Becca keep her arms around her mate's torso.

The day was getting so much better. But this moment topped it all.

Juana Makan

Nostalgia

After the 30-minute jog around the perimeter of the territory, Becca rested under a tall tree. Currently, she was in the training field. Early in the morning every day except on Sundays, warriors were always seen in training field. It was the discipline the Gamma had instilled on every warriors in training.

This was the situation that Becca witnessed at that time of the day.

Her father, Gamma Seth, was always leading the training.

"We're lucky today." Her father started.

"My daughter visited the pack after a long time. Might as well see if my trainings with you paid off."

Her eyes widen at the implication of his words. Having seen the reaction in her face, the gamma smirked.

She signed in resignation then, approached her father when he motioned her to come over.

"Dad, I'm a little rusty. It has been a while since I went through a hand-to-hand combat." She whispered when she stood beside him.

"I know but you are my daughter. I know about the rendezvous you and Remus had in the hill the other time."

She raised her head and gaped at him in shock.

"I know what happened in the hill eight years ago." He added sadly.

"I'm fine, daddy."

"I know." He pulled her closer and kissed her head. He turned to the warriors who were watching their interaction. Their faces were a mix of anticipation and challenge. However, Becca was having cold feet.

"Greg."

Gamma Seth called out.

A buff guy separated from the crowd. He was a bald man with a physique that showed he trained well. He stood taller than Becca but shorter than the gamma.

He stopped in front of them then eyed Becca. From the looks he was giving, he was already calculating the capability of his opponent.

"I'm doomed." She muttered under her breath.

"Don't let me down, baby girl." Gamma Seth said before stepping back.

Becca swallowed as she stared at Greg. He nodded at her.

"Can I be afraid now?" Becca asked her wolf.

Instead of supporting her, Lucy laughed like a freaking hyena.

"This is a hand-to-hand combat. Do not transform into your wolf." Gamma Seth announced. Mixed reaction was heard in the throng of warriors.

"You're on your own, hooman." Lucy squeaked.

"Thanks, Lucy. I appreciate the support."

Anytime.

Becca groaned before turning her attention on her opponent when they started on rounding each other. Both of their knuckles were raised in front of their face. None of them showed emotion. None showed any weakness.

Greg approached her. His stance was wide. He threw a punch in her face which she avoided with ease.

He made another jab in her right but she put her right forearm in her face to avoid his hit. He seemed to expect the defense as he followed his move with a kick on the side targeting the ribs. However Becca caught his feet then slide her palm until she seized his ankle. She gave him a straight punch in the nose after she secured the grip she had on his foot. He staggered then covered his face with his hands. If not for

Becca holding his ankle, he would have been sprawled on the ground. She did not wait for him to recover. She granted him a right hook. He lost his because he had only one foot on the ground, she then released two consecutive right kicks. He swayed as Becca let go of his ankle. She delivered a roundhouse kick and watched him stumble before he plummeted to the ground. Breathing heavily, she relaxed her stance while he lay on his back.

She dropped to her knees beside him but he remained motionless.

She slapped his face gently but made sure to avoid touching his bleeding nose as well as his swollen jaw. Becca disregarded the voices coming from the throng of warriors.

"Can you open your eyes?"

He did and blinked a few times. He frowned when he saw her hovering by his side.

"What happened?" He asked followed by a wince.

"You think you can stand?"

Becca asked.

"Maybe."

She helped him up as they walked towards the nearby bench. He still looked shaken.

"You have a crazy punch." He complained.

She sent him an easy smile as she steadily held him. She sat beside him as they turned to the training field. Gamma Seth was giving instruction to the trainees. With a proud smile, her father drew near them. "How are you feeling, Greg?"

"Like I was run over by a truck, sir."

Her dad chuckled.

"Do you need to be in the infirmary?"

"No, sir. My ego can no longer take the humiliation. I'll be fine in a couple of minutes." He responded half smiling, half wincing.

"Your daughter knows how to throw a punch where it matters, sir." Gamma Seth smirked. He turned to his daughter wearing a smug face.

"Rusty, huh."

She pouted at her father.

"You owe me breakfast, old man."

He laughs out loud before turning to the awaiting warriors in training.

"Combat training resumes this afternoon. Breakfast on me."

Whistles and cheerful hollers roared in the field.

Some were already running towards the cafeteria while others followed.

"Are you sure you don't want to see my mate, Greg?" Her father asked again.

"Yes, sir. I'll accept the free meal though."

A clap on the back later, they left Greg on his own as he nursed his bruised body and ego. They made their way to the cabin as Seth recapped the sparring that took place in the field. Noting the cheerful tone of his voice, he was in every way proud of his daughter. After her shower, Becca and her father marched their way to the cafeteria. A few of the trainees that were present in the field are still in the place.

"Welcome back, Little miss."

"Good morning, Mrs. Bennett." She greeted back when she saw the middle-aged woman at the counter.

"Are you still a hot choco person?" Mrs Bennett asked.

"Yes, ma'am, but I need a little boost today. Brewed coffee please."

Beaming at her, the old woman gets her drink. She added two cubes of brown sugar. Both she and her dad ordered the breakfast special which consisted of hash brown, scrambled eggs and bacon. They also asked for additional hash brown.

They were teasing each other as they ate when Alpha Remus entered the area. He was engaged in a conversation with a petite, white-haired woman. The half full cafeteria suddenly turned quiet. Tension surrounded the place. Becca noticed that her father turned grim.

"Are you alright?" She asked.

He took a deep breath then motioned at the woman accompanying the alpha.

"That is the witch contacted by the former alpha Luke. She is part of the Wit Blanche coven. Alpha Luke trusts her to help the pack against the group that attacked recently."

"Is she any good?" Becca inquired.

"I was told that she is an elder."

"Really?" Becca glanced at the witch when the Gamma nodded.

She was chewing on her second hash brown when she saw the witch say something at the alpha. Remus simply nodded his head to whatever the woman told him.

Becca continued watching the woman as she left the alpha. The petite woman marched toward their table. Gamma Seth straightened as the visiting witch approached.

"I'm famished."

Becca grinned when the witch grabbed the hash brown from her plate. She sat beside the tall woman as she finished the finger food in three bites.

"You know each other?" Her father asked.

"Yes, dad." Becca mumbled.

The petite woman continued snatching food from her plate. Becca offered her coffee, too.

The father and daughter watched the witch eat with gusto. The woman appeared ravenous.

"The last meal I had was the lunch yesterday. Aside from the pizza I got from Jakey, I haven't eat again. Your current alpha is very thorough." Mira blurted.

"You want more?"

"I'm good, babe. Your portion is big enough for two." The petite woman beamed at her before drinking the coffee in two gulps.

"You put two packets of sugar again." Mira complained while Becca laughed.

"Would you like to tell me something, Becca?" Her father interrupted.

Still smiling, she turned to her father.

"Dad, this is Mira Doue. She is my mate."

Show-Off

Becca wanted to laugh but it wasn't the proper thing to do at moments like this. Currently, she was sitting beside Mira on the dinner table at her parents' house.

On her right sits her father, Gamma Seth; the head of the family. In front of her sat her mother while Jake sat facing Mira. The chairs in the six-sitter table were vacant.

"Folks, are we going to eat or stay on having a staring contest?" Jake said, breaking the tension.

Becca was supposed to bring Mira last night at dinner to meet her parents. Unfortunately, her mate did not make it since she had a very long meeting with the alpha. Instead of Mira joining Becca to sleep with her in her family's cabin, she opted to sleep in the pack house.

Her work ended later than expected.

Olive, her mother, made a fake cough then beamed at every one before turning to Mira.

"Would you like some salad, dear?"

"Yes, please."

Mira replied cheerfully.

"When did you meet?" Seth asks Becca as Olive serves food into his plate.

Mira proceeded to put salad in her plate too then passed the bowl to Becca.

"Just recently, dad. I work in her company."

"You owned La Belle Scents?" Jake uttered in surprise. Mira beamed at the young man.

"Yes, Jakey."

"How do you and Luke know each other?" Becca's father asks again.

"Mira, please don't think that we do not like you for our daughter. I'm very happy that she found you." Her mom added.

"I'm glad I found her, too. Thank you, Mrs. Jackman."

Her mate sent a smile to the pack doctor before turning her attention back to the gamma.

"I'm friends with Luke's dad, Seth."

"Alpha Lander?"

The petite woman nodded.

"I helped him in his issues with his fake mate."

"Alpha Lander is Alpha Remus' gramps, right?" Jake interjected.

The glass of water he was supposed to drink remained suspended a few inches away from his mouth. As Becca chuckled, the frown on her parents face deepened. Despite the pinch she received on her side from her sweet mate, she was not able to stop the giggles coming out from her mouth.

"Folks, Mira is older than the two of you combine." She cleared.

"And I don't care."

"You're old?" Jake yelled.

"Yes, Jakey. Respect your elders, baby boy." Mira added with a grin.

"You're older than Dad." Jake yelled out again.

"Stop rubbing my age on my face, pup." Seth interjected.

"The mushroom is old." Jake muttered in a sing-song way. He cracked up while glancing at the witch.

"Babe, can I do something to your brother?" Mira whispered.

Becca nodded and watched what her mate was about to do. The sound of laughter stopped. However, Jake was still laughing. The three of them gaped at him. Her parents were looking at him wide-eyed while Becca beamed at her smirking mate. Mira doing her voodoo magic fascinates her. Jake straightened, suddenly realizing what was happening. He closed his mouth when he saw their faces. He must have noticed the terror in his parents' eyes. He tried saying something but realized that no sound came out.. He stood up abruptly then glanced at his parents in distress.

"Babe, please bring his voice back." Becca pleaded while giggling

"Because you said please." Mira replied.

"I'm going to strangle you with my bare hands!" Jake screamed.

"I liked him quiet, babe." Mira frowned.

"Stop it, Jacob."

The gamma exclaimed before his son could reach his daughter's newly found mate. Jake no longer joined the conversation as the dinner progressed. However, he kept on giving Mira an eye. On the other hand, Seth and Olive warmed up to their daughter's mate. They were both thankful that their daughter has finally moved on. No one mentioned about the first mate since Jacob has no knowledge about it. Seth has been indifferent about the rejection that his daughter has to go through a few years back.

"I had fun. Thank you for the delicious dinner." Mira uttered as they finished their coffee.

"It was nice meeting you, too." Becca's mum replied.

"The pleasure is all mine, Olive. If you wish to know about the childhood tales of your husband, please don't hesitate to ask."

Beaming, Olive winked at the witch.

"That would be a good reason for a girl's night out."

With a smile painted on her lips, Becca watched her mate and mother getting cozy. She felt her father's arm on her shoulder.

"I'm glad you found your second mate." He whispered. "She might be older but she's okay."

She chuckled. "Thanks, dad."

"Fossil." Jake muttered in his breath.

Becca reach for her mate's hand before she could do something to her brother again. After saying their goodbye, Mira and Becca left the cabin. They traced the road towards the pack house where Mira stays. Her witch of a mate would have stayed with her but she was told by the woman herself that she was currently working on a potion that needed her full attention. The mere presence of Becca would interfere with the process. Becca's objections and promises of behaving fell on deaf ears.

"See you at breakfast?" Mira pouted.

The petite woman does that whenever she is thinking.

"Late breakfast perhaps?" She added.

"Sure. Call me?" Becca replied.

They stopped in front of the door to the room that Mira occupied. "I miss you, babe. Can we go home together when this is over?" Becca pleaded.

"It depends on how long I'm going to stay here. My leave from the office is coming to an end."

"Can you extend it?" Mira asked.

"This sudden leave is almost impossible if not for your threats. Janessa already gave me an earful before I left." She recalled smiling.

Mira pulled the tall woman and encircled her arms around the werewolf's torso. Becca hugged her closer before kissing her head.

"Thank you for forcing me to come back home." Becca muttered sincerely.

"I knew that you missed them a lot." The petite woman whispered before lifting her face. "Besides, I wanted to know the guy who rejected you."

One brow raised, Becca replied.

"He's in the past, babe."

"I want to thank him. Please?" She shook her head.

"Are you still into him? Is that why you came back?" Mira said bitterly while letting her go. Her glare focus on the tall woman.

Becca stared at those beautiful blue eyes. "This heart is yours, Mira. I'm yours."

The witch looked away. A smile formed at the petite woman's lips.

"Fine. Kiss me so I could go back to the cabin."

Mira demanded and returned to her arms. A peck on the lips later, Becca walked back to her parents' cabin. A smile glued to her lips as she looked forward for tomorrow's events.

Under Dog

From the entrance Becca watched her mate pacing from one corner of the house to another. Mira has this small satchel in her hand.

The small woman was muttering in her breath words that Becca could not comprehend. As the witch murmurs she also scatters powdered substances that she dug up from the satchel.

Becca returned to the kitchen when her mate disappeared from her sight. She must be in the other corners of the house doing the same voodoo magic she did in the front of the cabin.

When she went back to the front door, Mira was already there. Holding two mugs of coffee in hand, she moves towards the four sitter garden seat. She placed the mugs on top of the gray marbled table then sat on one of the chairs made of steel. Becca pulled the petite woman towards her. Still on her feet, Mira faced her. The tall woman noticed the distress on her mate's face.

"Tell me." Becca asked.

"Something is going to happen."

"Did you tell alpha Remus?" Mira nodded.

"Dad is with him. They must be going through a plan."

"Where's Jakey?"

"He's on patrol."

Becca guided her worried mate to sit on her lap. Mira pressed her face against the tall woman's neck as the later surrounded her arms around her mate's torso.

"Are you going to let Lucy out?"

"If I have to." Becca answered.

"Don't."

"Why?"

"Just don't."

"Alright."

Mira stayed on her lap as they sipped their coffee. Mira was starting to relax when she suddenly straightened. The witch stood up and opened the satchel attached in her wrist. She put her hands inside. When it took it out, there was a dried heather in between her fingers. She pulled Becca until they stood side by side then put the dried heather inside the pocket of the female werewolf's shorts.

"Do not let Lucy out no matter what happens. Defend yourself in any means necessary without letting your wolf out." Mira commanded.

Becca frowned. Lucy was protesting in her head. Her upper cranium was hurting because of the objections her wolf is making. She did not know that she had closed her eyes until she felt Mira touching her face. Understanding and determination were written on her face.

"Lucy, baby." Her mate called out. Mira knew that her wolf was having an issue inside her head. Becca blinked a few times before opening her eyes. Lucy was still trying to oppose their mate but eventually settled down when Mira kept on caressing her face.

"Please let Becca reign tonight. Promise me."

"Alright." The taller woman said in almost whiny voice which was not her.

"Thank you, baby."

Mira finally smiled. She gave her a peck on the lips.

Lucy, on the other hand, calmed down with a wide grin on her snout.

"They are here."

Mira suddenly said.

"Where?" Becca panicked.

"At the east border."

"Can we go to the infirmary? I want to see my mother."

Hands intertwined, they ran towards the pack house.

They found warriors surrounding the building. With the expression on their faces, they knew how serious the situation was is. This also showed that alpha Remus came prepared.

"Alpha." They greeted.

Remus nodded at them. He did not say a word seeing them together.

"East border needs reinforcement." He uttered. Six warriors ran towards the said direction.

"It's a distraction, Alpha Remus. More are coming from the South." Mira disclosed.

"Gamma Seth is leading the warriors there." Remus bit back.

"They have the witch at the South, alpha."

Becca stilled. Her father was in great danger!

"Lead the way, babe. Let's meet that bitch."

Without waiting for the alpha's command, Becca ran towards the direction where her father was, Mira in tow.

"Don't you have a broom or something?" Becca asked when they were in the woods.

"That's so old school."

The tall woman felt a tight grip on her on her palm before a strong gush of wind slapped her on the face. Becca staggered on her feet when the biting wind disappeared. A little disoriented, she looked around. The fight was still on-going. Mira was already making hand gestures. Bodies were being thrown on the ground or on the trunks of the trees. Standing on guard, she stayed beside her mate. She noticed that the attackers were in their human forms while the members of the Cloudless Moon pack were in their wolf forms. Flicking her hands, human bodies kept on piling on the ground. Her witch mate was quite busy.

"Come out, witch." Mira muttered.

Growling continued but the fight ceased. The attackers stayed on their feet as they watched Mira. They finally understood that the petite woman beside her was their biggest opponent.

"Show yourself, you perpetrator of this petty ambush." Her mate taunted.

When two men walked towards them , Mira moved her left wrist and two ended up colliding against a tree. They fell on the ground unconscious. The six werewolves surrounding them moaned in pain. Becca was about to approach the gray wolf when Mira stopped her.

"That's my dad!" Becca yelled.

Her mate sighed before nodding. She ran to her father who was lying on his side. He growled in pain like the other werewolves.

"Oh, no! Not on my watch."

Becca cradled her father's head when he stopped moving. She saw him blink as he breaths heavily. When Becca glanced at her mate, Mira's attention was on the edge of the territory. As she turned to the same direction, a red haired woman was standing beside an old tree. The said woman looked younger. Fear was also visible in her face. The red haired woman turned to Becca and flicked her hand but nothing seemed to happened. She flicked her hand again but Becca remained untouched.

"Where is your commander?" Mira yelled.

The fear in the young witch's face turns to anger. Becca noticed that her lips were moving. Fearing for her mate's life, Becca turned to Mira again. Her witch looked pissed. She made a pushing gesture on her hand before waving her hand from left to right. She did the left and right motion a few times. Becca found herself watching the young witch's body swaying from the left to the right. Just like Mira's hand did.

"Babe, contain this woman please."

Becca placed her father's head on the ground before approaching the young witch. The red haired appeared disoriented. The young woman was still swaying back and forth like a rag doll. When Becca stopped, the swaying stopped, too. The red haired crumpled on the ground weakly. A rope appeared beside the young witch and Becca used it to tie up the woman. She was about to carry the witch when it disappeared. She glanced at Mira.

"She ain't that lucky, wolfie." Mira grinned.

She looked down before smiling. Her mate's possessive nature has no specific place and time. And she and Lucy loved it.

Remnant Of The Past

Series of meetings welcomed Becca when she returned to work. She did not receive any query from her immediate boss since her leave of absence was not extended. The reports that she asked for from the account officers around the State poured into her emails the first day that Becca came back.

As punishment for the short vacation she had, she went home late for three straight days. Work had piled up on her table the days that she was absent from the office. Mira was in the living room when Becca arrived at her apartment. She placed the box of pizza on top of the table for Becca.

"Freshen' up, babe."

The tall woman nodded before she headed to her bedroom. Fifteen minutes later, she came back to her mate. Mira was in the kitchen. The aroma of the cheesy pizza was in the air. She pulled a chair and sat beside the petite woman. She poured water into both of their glasses then spread chili sauce on the two slices of pizza.

"Everything alright?" Becca asked when she noticed that her girlfriend was not her usual bubbly self. This is the first time that they were seeing each other again after their short rendezvous in the Cloudless Moon pack. Though they went back to the city together, they got separated at the airport.

"The young witch that attacked the pack, she has been on my mind lately." Mira replied solemnly.

"Should I be worried?"

Mira glanced at her. The petite woman threw her a piece of mushroom when she saw the playful grin on her face.

Becca chuckled. She pulled her mate and guide her to sit on her lap. She put her arms around her middle.

"What's bothering you?"

"I smell vampire in her."

"And?"

"She is mated to one. But I also smelled a familiar one."

"How many vampires are we talking about?"

"I don't know." She kissed the temple of her worried mate.

"Are you thinking that a vampire is behind the attacks on my pack?" Mira nodded.

"An old foe."

"What do you mean?"

"I need to meet with Lander."

"Alpha Lander is in Africa now. He's spending most of his time travelling with his mate ever since his son accepted the alpha position." Becca informed.

"He needs to know that he's back."

"Who?"

"Rudolf."

"Rudolf?" Mira nodded.

"I have to go back to the pack. Everyone will be in danger."

"I need to tell Janessa to find me a temporary replacement." Becca replied.

The petite woman faced her. A smile formed in her lips.

"You're coming with me?" Mira asked.

"Of course. This isn't about me anymore. I have to be there with you. Who is Rudolf to you?"

"He is the real mate of the woman who introduced herself as the fake mate of the former alpha Lander."

"What?"

"He will be looking for me and the descendants of Alpha Lander. By going back to the Cloudless Moon pack, I just re-affirmed that I am still connected to the pack."

"Why is he doing this?" Becca queried.

"He wanted a land from the pack. He used his mate to lure the alpha so that he could have the territory. It was unfortunate for him that I am an acquaintance of the young alpha Lander."

"How did you and Alpha Lander meet?"

"He tried to woe me. That old man was a flirt in his days."

"He's not your ex, right?"

"Of course not, silly."

Becca sighed, grateful that the former alpha was not a former lover of the love of her life.

"Speaking of which, why haven't you mark me yet?" Mira asked.

The tall woman swallowed. The full attention of her mate is on her. Her heart began pounding faster.

"What's stopping you, Becca?" Mira asked worriedly. Becca looked away..

"Are you still thinking of your first mate?" Mira spat.

Becca turned back to her mate. The woman was glaring furiously at her.

"Of course not, babe!"

"Then what, Jackman?!"

Mira stood up. She placed both her hands in her hips as she glowered at the werewolf.

"Are you still having doubts in this bond?"

Becca grabbed both of her hands in hers and squeezed them softly.

"I don't have reservations in this relationship. I trust you, Mira."

"Then why?"

She took a deep breath and stared at her baby blues. "I'm doubting myself. I may not be good enough for you."

"You're enough for me." Mira whispered.

"Is it because I'm an elder?"

"I'm a nobody, babe. Being an elder is one thing. But you're the head of the Wit Blance coven."

The petite woman's eyes widen in surprise. Becca smiled sadly and caressed the face of the witch. Mira did not tell her that she was the current coven leader. But from their previous conversations, she learned that Mira was part of the Wit Blance coven or the White hair coven. Knowing that Mira almost gave the company to Janessa and from the complaints that she heard from her good friend and boss, it was enough confirmation that her mate was busy doing something else. That something else is another huge responsibility.

"You're a strong witch, babe. Very strong. No matter how you and Janessa banter, she respects you. Your presence demanded respect. The aura that you emit, it's powerful." She explained. "I can't equate to that."

"Are you rejecting me because I'm powerful?" The witch uttered in a small but poignant voice.

It was Becca's turned to glare.

"Who said I'm rejecting you?"

"Then what?"

The tall woman cupped the witch's face in between her palms. She stared at her beautiful blue eyes.

"I'm just trying to lay out my insecurities. Who said that I'm letting you go, woman? I'm not letting another mate go. Not this time." Mira smiled.

"Then do something about that, wolfie."

"Are you sure? I'm just a normal werewolf, Mira." "You're my werewolf. I'll be strong enough for the both of us."

They stared at each other. Her blues meet brown eyes.

"Are you not going to kiss me, Becca?"

"You're a demanding woman. Are you even aware of that?"

"I've been told so. My rank requires command too."

"We'll see who's boss."

Becca closed the distance between them. Mira immediately opened her mouth to meet Becca's. As the tall woman surrounded her arms around her mate, the petite woman put her hands on Becca's shoulders. They both kissed and fought for dominance since no one seemed to back down. Becca stood up. Her hands slide down to the back of Mira's knees. As she lifted the petite woman, Mira encircled her legs around Becca's waist. Their kiss did not waver.

"Are you sure about this?" The tall woman asked when their lips parted to breath. Both of them were already breathing heavily. The petite woman nodded. Becca pecked her lips again before marching them towards the bedroom.

'At last!' Lucy sighed before yapping in her head.

Morning After

The murmurs in her surrounding woke Becca from her deep slumber. She smiled when it was her mate that she saw when she opened her eyes. Mira was still unaware of her surroundings. The witch was sitting beside her in bed. The light coming from the tinted windows created a glow around Mira's face.

The petite woman's eyes were closed as she muttered incomprehensible words in her breath. She was also doing some hand motions on top of Becca. The tall woman stayed on her back as she stared at her beautiful mate. A smile appeared on her lips as she caught a glimpse of the traces of last night's episode. Peeking out of the robe that Mira was wearing were the hickeys that Becca intentionally left behind. The previous night had been wonderful. She had finally claimed her mate. Despite the insecurity, Mira made her forget that she had flaws. Mira made her realized that she was enough. Last night was perfect. A kiss on the lips made her return to the moment. Mira was hovering above her. Gentleness plastered in her face. Becca sent her mate a contented smile.

"Are you done with your voodoo magic?" Mira caressed her cheek before nodding.

"You'll be protected by my magic. My scent is mixed with yours, too."

Becca grinned. "Basically, we now smell the same?"

"Yes."

"I like that."

Her index finger traced the skin exposed at the center of the robe. Mira swallowed when her fingers reached the valley between her ample breast.

"Anything else you'd like?" Becca asked.

"A lot, actually. But we can start with this." Mira said then pulled the loosely tied belt of the robe. It opens to an appetizing feast that Becca's tongue lavishly tasted last night. Her finger caught one pinkish nipple. She found Mira biting her lower lip. She lifted her head and seized the other nipple with her mouth. The sexy moan of her mate brought Becca a form of gratification. Knowing that she could make her mate release a beautiful sound of pleasure. She latched on the nipples harder until Mira grabbed her short hair. Becca put her other hand inside the caressed her mate's back until she felt the goose bumps on her skin.

"Babe."

Mira breathed out.

"Hmm." She murmured.

"Babe."

"What do you want, babe?"

"No more playing. I want you inside me." Mira moaned.

"Still demanding, I see. Let me show you who's boss."

Becca pulled her petite mate back to bed. She hovered on top of her and kissed her full on the mouth. All the while, her hands where having its own feast. Hours later, Becca and Mira marched into the office building of La Belle Scents. She had their coffee on one hand while the other was intertwined with Mira's. They were the only people in the elevator. Becca proceeded to her office while Mira goes to the office of the marketing director. Each having a coffee in their hand. A boost of caffeine would do them good since they had a busy night.

She was in the middle of a meeting with the account officer of the Vintage Place, one of the malls in the State, when Janessa and Mira turned up in her small office. Becca and the account officer greeted the bosses. The account manager wrapped up the meeting before ending the conversation via zoom.

"What can I help you with, ladies?" Becca turned her chair to the two witches. Janessa already made herself comfortable at the only extra chair in the small office while Mira stands beside the table.

"Are you going back to your pack?" Janessa asked. The tall woman glanced at her mate before nodding. She was no longer surprised with Janessa's knowledge of the pack and her identity. Mira may have already told her about it and the current predicament of the Cloudless Moon Pack. Her mate may have already told her niece who they were to each other.

"I would like to ask for my temporary replacement. I don't know how long I'm going to stay in the pack." She disclosed freely. The cat was out of the bag, anyway.

"Sounds dangerous."

"It is. There is a possibility that you'll be managing the coven, too." Mira interjected in a serious manner.

"That's not acceptable, Aunt Mira. Is it not enough that I have to manage this company that you have to put the responsibility of the coven in my shoulder?" Janessa yelled.

"Janessa, I have my full confidence in you."

"Stop right there, old woman." The young witch put her palm out. She turned to Becca.

"Tell your girlfriend to stay alive. I plan to live older before I take over the coven."

Becca smiled at the young boss stressful outburst.

"We plan to stay alive until we get enough of each other."

Janessa made a face.

"Mates. Duh!"

That being said, her young boss knew who Mira is to her. Beaming, Mira made herself comfortable in her lap. With a contented sigh, Becca pulled her mate closer to her body. She sniffed her neck in a subtle manner. Her mate still smells of honeysuckle but she now has a hint of newly chopped woods. It was said to be the hint of smell every member of the Cloudless Moon pack have in common.

"You smell a little like me." She whispered.

"Mated. Damn!"

Becca and Mira chuckled at the other woman.

"I'm putting one of the account supervisors in your place. Have her train by tomorrow. Don't leave until she knows her new responsibility."

"Yes, ma'am."

Without another word Janessa left them in their own little world. Becca glanced at the bandage in her mate's neck. She placed it in the morning after their shower. Last night, they consummated the second step to the mating process, the sexual intercourse. They also progressed to the third step, the marking. Though they have long accepted the mating bond as the first step on the mating process, Becca wanted to get to know each other before they proceeded to the next two steps. It was worth the wait.

"Your neck still painful?" Becca asked.

"Not anymore."

"We should put something in it to avoid infection."

"I have something in my house."

"Great! Now, can I get back to work? I need to prepare everything for my substitute."

"Your job is a hindrance between us."

Becca grinned at her mate's complaint.

"I have to keep my job for the both of us. You said that you don't have the money to sustain us both."

She heard the petite woman huff. She kissed Mira in the cheek and embraced her tighter.

"I love you."

A smile painted on Mira's lips but did not utter the words back. Instead, she grips the hands on her middle and laid more comfortably in the arms of her mate.

Face-Off

"F**K!"

Despite the disoriented state, Becca clearly heard Jake swearing. She and Mira just arrived at her parents' cabin. From the airport, they the most secluded area in order for Mira to use her ability. This way they would be home faster than going to the pack territory through land.

"Good morning, Jakey." Mira teased.

"Must you do that? Freaking mushroom!" Jake yelled.

"Help me with your sister, will you?" Mira snapped.

Becca felt two pairs of hand holding her before her ass settled in a couch. She closed her eyes hoping the dizziness would subside. This is the second time that Mira used her ability to teleport with Becca in tow. However, the further the distance, the person inside a teleportation activity would experience a longer time feeling seismic movement and being slapped in the face with strong winds.

"Can we use broom next time?" Becca asked as she massage her temple.

"That is so old school, babe."

When Becca open her eyes, she was already in the living room of her parents' cabin. Mira was sitting beside her in the couch and Jake was crouched down in front of her.

"You okay, Becky?" Jake asked.

"I will feel much better after a while. Where's the parents?'

"At work. I just finished patrol duty. The alpha did not ease the security. There has been minor attacks since both of you left."

Jake stood up and occupied another chair. Becca blinked a few times. The lightheadedness she felt finally eased. Truth be told, she did not want to experience that again. Next time they would take the long drive.

"Aren't you tired or dizzy?' She asked her mate.

"I'm used to teleporting."

"Good for you then. Where are our things?"

"In your room. They arrived earlier." Becca nodded before turning to her brother.

"Did you have your breakfast yet?"

"Yes. I lost my appetite, anyway. Tell your mate to stop popping up anywhere." He glared at the woman beside her.

"That mate is here." Mira snapped.

"I don't care, fossil."

"Stop it, babe." Becca groaned.

"I'm starting to like your brother very much."

"I know."

Becca stood up. The world was not moving anymore. Feeling steady on her feet she grabbed her mate's hand and dragged her towards the door.

"See you later, Jake." Becca called.

"So long that mushroom is out of my personal space."

"Remain vigilant, baby boy."

"Shut up, fossil."

Before Mira could say her piece, Becca closed the front door. Without glancing at the petite woman, Becca knew that her mate was possibly pouting beside her. Not having the last word was so not her. They marched toward the pack house. They have to report to the alpha that they were inside the territory. Though Becca is still a member of the

Cloudless Moon Pack, Alpha Remus knows that she lives in the city. Mira is welcome in the territory but she has to request for the alpha's permission to stay. The same goes for Becca.

After a warning knock, the mated couple enter the private office of Alpha Remus. The alpha leader was doing something on his laptop when they entered. He stopped typing when he saw them. He stood up and motioned for them to approach.

"Good morning, Alpha."

"Good morning. The patrol did not notify that both of you were here." Remus replied.

"It was my fault." Mira admitted.

Remus nodded in understanding. He extended his hand for a handshake. Both of them accepted it.

"It is good to see both of you."

He sat again while the two women occupied the seats in front of his table.

"I need to talk to your grandparents." Mira disclosed.

"Grandpa Lander is on vacation. I'm afraid he and grams are out of reach at the moment."

"He needs to cut his vacation short. Please tell him that Rudolf strikes again. He would understand."

Alpha Remus stared at the witch. It was clear that he has objections. The alpha got his mobile phone from the side drawer. He pressed a few keys before putting the communication device on top of the table. The phone rings on loud speaker. Three rings later, the person on the other line answered.

"Remus." The gruff voice said.

"Gramps. How's vacation?"

"What's wrong?" The former alpha said directly.

Alpha Remus glanced at the witch before responding.

"Rudolf strikes again."

A few seconds of silence passed before the former alpha spoke again.

"Is Mira there?" Alpha lander asks.

"Yes." The petite woman answered while Alpha Remus nodded.

"He's back, isn't he?"

"Yes."

"I'll be home in two days."

"See you soon, Lander."

The three of them sighed when the call ended. They stared at the innocent device.

Remus cleared his throat before he muttered.

"Both of you are welcome to stay."

"Thank you, Alpha. She will be staying with me in my parents' cabin." Becca replied.

The alpha nodded. He stood up and shook their hands again.

"Congratulations on your mating, by the way."

"Thank you, Alpha Remus."

They left the alpha's office and proceeded to the cafeteria. The thoughts of the reason why they were here in pack was thrown out of the window at the moment. For now, their growling stomach leads. It was a few minutes before 9AM. There were only a few people inside the cafeteria. Becca advanced to the counter to get their food while Mira proceeded to find a seat for them.

"Coffee for my lovely mate." Becca said as she placed the tray of food on top of the table. She placed the coffee beside her mate before putting everything else on the table.

"Thank you." Mira inhaled the aroma of the freshly brewed black coffee.

"More hash browns, too?" Becca smiles. She ensured that she had added them. Mira and her both love hash brown. Breakfast was peaceful. No one bothered them since pack members were still wary of the presence of the witch. They were almost done eating when a group of warriors in training enter the dining area. The training must have been dismissed.

"Gamma Seth is really meticulous." One of them uttered.

"But he's fair and give free meals." Another one added as the others agreed with him.

"But not today though."

"I wonder where his daughter is though. I heard she's in the city working in a big company."

"She chose the life in the human population other than live in the pack. No one knows why she left."

"She was in college when she left according to Jake. Her sudden return was a few weeks ago."

"Whatever you say, man. She's a badass in my eyes. She put Greg on his ass."

The banter continued as the other warriors pitched into the conversation.

"You fought against a warrior, huh. And you won." Mira said with a smirk.

"It was pure luck, babe."

"You always sell yourself short, Becca. Truth be told, you're a freaking badass."

The shifter sent her mate a smile. The petite woman smiled back. It was clear that the witch was very proud of her. That was enough for Becca.

The Encounter

Becca pushed her brother when she reached him. In turn, Jake stumbled on his feet but immediately regained his balance. He pulled his sister's hair before running ahead.

It was six o'clock in the morning and the siblings were running round the border of the territory.

Last night, she and Jake decided to run early today.

As they ran, they kept on having fun with each other. They poked, pushed and even kicked each other just to take the lead. There was even a point when Becca found herself on the ground. To retaliate, she jumped on Jake's back and made him run for ten minutes carrying her.

"I've never had fun like this for a while." Jake breathed out while sitting beside his sister. They sat beside a creek. This is their pit stop before going back. Less than ten minutes later, the youngest Jackman stood up and removed his top. He walked towards the creek and washed his face. He might have felt warmer because he decided to sit down at the flowing water. He tapped the water with his open palms and begun to laugh like a little boy. He scoops the water and tosses it to his resting sister. Instead of feeling mad, Becca giggled. She walked towards the water and did the same to her brother. Their laughter echoed all over the place. This was just like the old times but back then it was their parents who brought them here. They rode at their parents backs in their wolf form since during those times they were still unable to transform into their wolves.

"Oh, siblings."

They stopped. They were alerted by the unfamiliar voice. On the other side of the creek stood a tall man in his forties. He was alone. The creek is ten meters wide. It borders Cloudless Moon Pack and La Luna. The two pack has been in good terms for generations.

"What's a vampire doing in a werewolf territory?" Becca snarled.

"Sightseeing, perhaps." He followed it with chuckle. Jake growled behind her.

"See you around."

With a blink of an eye, the vampire was gone. Playfulness gone. The siblings looked around for intruder. When they saw no one, both of them got out of the creek. They looked at each other before running back home. Jake proceeded to the pack house. He ran to report the incident to the alpha. On the other hand, Becca ran home. There was no one at cabin. After taking a shower, Becca looked for her mobile phone. Mira was still asleep when she went for a run this morning with Jake. However, her mate was no longer in bed when she came back. There was a text message from her Mira saying that she has a meeting with the alpha. With a sigh, she marched toward the kitchen. The sun was not even in its brightest form but this happened. She got the things she needed from the cupboard. Might as well make breakfast, she thought. No one knows what is going to pop up any time today. A full stomach would help with whatever it is that is going to happen. Becca was flipping the last pancake when a pair of slim arms surrounded her torso. A smile formed on her lips. She placed the pancake on top of the others before grabbing the hand of her mate. She turned toward Mira.

"Good morning."

"Good morning, babe." She pecked her lips. She took hold of the plate that contain the pancakes and grabs her mate with the other. She puts the food on the table then guides Mira to one seat. She places two mugs of coffee on the table before sitting beside Mira. Her mate beamed at her before pouring honey on the pancakes. If Becca's pancakes were swimming in syrupy sweetness, Mira has very little.

"What happened in the creek, babe?" Mira questioned. Becca sighed before turning to her mate.

"There was a vampire on the other side of the creek."

"La Luna has been an ally of Cloudless Moon Pack, right?"

Becca nodded. She did not bother to ask how her mate learned about that fact. She would not be surprised if, her mate had a hand in creating a good relationship between the two packs.

"Remus already called the attention of the nearby territory. He told the alpha about the vampire in his border." Mira disclosed after she had her first bite.

"Do you know the vampire, babe?"

Mira nodded. "He's an old foe."

"Rudolf?"

"Yes." Mira sipped her coffee before she continued.

"He might have an idea that you're my mate." Becca grabs her mate's hand and intertwines it with hers. She smiles at her mate.

"I'm fine, babe."

"I know."

"He was not with anyone when we saw him."

"He might be scouting the perimeter. That guy is cunning." Mira replied.

"What's the plan of the alpha?"

"For now, he has put additional wolves in the borders. The other pack will do the same. At this moment, Rudolf's troop cannot enter your pack because we have the witch but who knows when he will find another one." Becca kissed the back of Mira's palm. "I believe that we can beat his ass. This pack has the best witch."

Her mate beamed at her. "As long as you're safe I am the strongest witch."

"I promise not to do stupid things."

The petite woman chuckled. "I will hold on to that promise. Besides, you make the best coffee and pancake in the world."

"It's made of love, babe."

"Could this day be any better?"

Both of them turned to Jake. He was standing beside the wall in the kitchen entrance. He had no shirt. He left it in the creek. But he was no longer wet.

"Breakfast, Jakey?"

"Please."

Her brother sat beside Mira. Becca got her brother a mug of coffee. He needed the boost of caffeine, too. When she returned to the table, she was not surprised when she found layers of pancakes in another plate. The bottle of honey was pouring itself on top of the pancakes. Amazement was written on her brother's face. The bottle of honey put itself back on the table. The plate slide towards Jake. Fork and knife followed and place themselves on each side. Becca put the mug in front of her brother.

"Bon appetite, baby boy." Mira smirked.

"Wow! Thank you."

Their conversation continued but on a lighter mood. The siblings recounted what happened in the creek with Mira. The witch did not say anything as they retold the lastminute details of the encounter. "He cannot enter the territory."

"What?"

"I made a warding spell in every border.

"Then why the hell did those rogues attacked the pack?" Jake shouted.

"Babe, your brother's voice can irritate the hell out of me." Mira turned to her as she pouted. "Don't seal my mouth, fossil. It's a valid question." Becca nodded as she glanced at her mate. She continued drinking her coffee. The pancakes were gone from her plate in no time.

"The warding spell I made were for vampires and werewolves. The witch we captured helped them enter the territory. If you noticed, the rogues that attacked the pack were in human form." Jake stopped eating. He went silence for a few seconds before he nodded.

"The witch can attack a big number of werewolves in an area but she can't when in human form." "Why? I mean, you know. Are her powers very selective?" Jake asked.

"She's still a young witch. She was a part of garmir kakhard coven in Armania."

"Gar—what?"

"The red witch coven."

"Oh? And you're a white witch." Jake said and continue eating. He frowned when none of them refuted his statement. He gazed at the both of them.

"You are?" Mira nodded.

"I thought the hair was just for a show."

Becca laughed in her seat. She continued drinking from her mug that does not seem to get empty. She glanced at her mate and when their eyes met, she made a tossing gesture with her mug. Mira sent her a smile.

Alpha Lander

More than 50 years ago. Mira watched the members of Cloudless Moon pack as she walked around. Currently, she was inside a werewolf territory. She has been visiting this pack for a while now. She met Lander Franklin, the alpha of this pack, two years ago when she visited a human friend down town. The alpha tried to flirt with her but she ignored the werewolf. This made the young alpha to follow her like a lost puppy. She explained to the young alpha that she knew who and what he is. As expected, Lander was surprised. She told him that she will not accept the affection he offers since she knew that he has a mate waiting for him. From then on, friendship blossomed between them that Mira was able to visit him in the territory. Pack members were used to seeing her around.

"Good morning. Where can I find Alpha Lander?" She asked a woman when she arrived at the semi furnished pack house.

"He's in the infirmary." Surprised by the answer, she asked again.

"Where is the infirmary?" The woman pointed at the cabin not too far from where she was standing. She thanked the woman and sauntered toward the cabin. There was a bench on both sides of the open cabin. There were people loitering the area. At the far side, there was a single cot. An injured man was laying there. He has a piece of wood attached in his arm. His face was bruised. She turned left when she reached the man by the cot. More people were being treated. The medical aids were attending to people with severe injuries. She glanced again at the man on cot. His eyes were now open. She kneeled beside him.

"Do you know where Alpha Lander is?"

"He's in that room." He answered in a gruff voice.

Mira gazed at the closed door that the man pointed. She thanked him then knocked twice before opening the door. There was a single bed inside the room and the alpha is laying there when Mira entered. She pushed the curtain and opened the window. Fresh air filled into the room.

"At last, a pleasing sight."
"Injured or not, flattery comes naturally from your mouth." She helped the wounded alpha to sit. She placed two pillows in his back. Lander has a long gash on his forehead. His left jaw was discolored. Both his forearms had several abrasions.

"What happened?"

"A group of vampires attacked the territory just before the sun showed up."

"Was there any casualty?"

"Four."

This might be the reason why there was a dismal aura surrounding the people when she entered the territory. She thought it was just too early for the pack to be very active on a Sunday.

"Did you capture anyone?"

The alpha shook his head.

"I'm sorry for your loss." Mira pressed Lander's hand in sympathy. The alpha responded with a sad smile.

"I should go and help the nurses. Their hands are full."

"Thank you, Mira."

That was the first of the several attacks in the pack. It was a great challenge for the young alpha. Lander made sure that the patrol was always on guard. The members of the pack that could fight were pushed to undergo warriors' training. It paid until suddenly the attacks stopped. However, the alpha did not lower his guard down. Mira visited the pack again a few months later. She came from down town. She came to pay her last respect to her human friend who died of severe pneumonia. Several children ran past her as she walked towards the pack house. They paid her no mind due to her familiarity. When she reached the office of the alpha, she knocked twice before turning the door knob. She was dumbfounded when saw the situation inside. She turned away.

"I'm sorry. I'll back later."

Lander chuckled.

"Come on in, Mira. Please."

She looked down. She gave them time to straightened themselves before she raised her eyes. Beside her Alpha friend there was a pretty woman. She was much taller than her five feet and two inches. The alpha put his arms around the woman's shoulder. Mira noticed the woman flinched from the gesture.

"I want you to meet my lovely mate, Elizabeth. Liz, this is my good friend, Mira. She is human but she knows of our existence."

"Hello, Mira." Elizabeth said in a small voice.

"Hello." They shook hands. She found Lander looking at his mate with those lovey dovey eyes lovers often have. She smiled to herself.

"I should go. I'll leave the two of you."

"Can I come with you? Lander has been trying to monopolize my time. Besides, he has a lot to do as an alpha should."

"Darling."

"Finish it then we'll have more time."

A sound of protest once more was heard from the young alpha. However, for what it's worth Mira did not bother looking at them as they turned silent.

"Bye, alpha." Mira then went outside to wait for Liz. The woman beamed at her when their eyes meet. She smiled back.

"Now, at least I've met another friend of his. Most of the people around him are men and warriors." Liz said as they walked away from the pack house.

"How did you two meet?"

"I was down town visiting a friend. We accidentally bumped into each other." Mira answered the tall woman.

"The same thing happened to us. Well, I slammed into him since I wasn't looking. However, what happened next was magical."

"Really?"

"Yes. Finally, I found the one the goddess has made for me."

Mira saw how her eyes sparkled when she said that. She did not see that when they were inside the alpha's office.

"Congratulations! Alpha Lander has been waiting for his mate." She said, instead.

"And he found me."

"Yes." Liz stopped walking just to stare at the petite woman.

"I hope you don't mind if I get jealous sometimes. Werewolves are naturally possessive."

"I understand. I know about mates." Mira assured.

"Good. Are you mated to one?" Liz asked.

Mira shook her head.

"A friend of mine is mated to a werewolf. She told me about it."

"Is she part of the pack?"

Mira went after her when Liz continued walking.

"She's not part of the pack. Her mate was part of another pack. They decided to build a family in the human population."

"Oh."

"How about you? From what pack are you?"

"I'm a rouge. I was on the run when Lander and I met."

"I'm sorry."

"It's okay. At least now I have him. I hope to stay that way."

Frowning, Mira peeked at the woman through her lashes. She looked away before Liz could see her face.

"Let's go to the training ground. We'll never know, you might find the man for you."

Mira sent her a smile before they followed the path towards the field.

The Caring Luna

Mira sat on the bench under an old tree. The tree stood proudly a few meters away from the infirmary. Whenever she was in the pack she always helped at the pack hospital. She likes aiding the medical personnel. She also gave them the ointments she made for any kind of wound. Suffice it to say, she added a little magic on it to accelerate the healing of any abrasions. Whenever they asked where she got the cream from, she told them that it was a family recipe. The medical aide smiles at her. They were still grateful that she had shared the remedy. They said that the salve was quite useful since the werewolves were often in the infirmary. They always have reasons to start a brawl. The sun was already down when Mira entered the pack house. Alpha Lander already assigned a room just for her whenever she visits. In fact, the room was situated on the far side of the Alpha's quarter.

Mira proceeded to the kitchen. Her stomach is already clamoring for sustenance since she forgot to eat lunch. She collected some herbs in the forest when she left the infirmary earlier. She had lots of fun since she found rare ones that she had a hard time finding in other areas. Truth be told, the satchel she was carrying was full when she returned to the pack house.

"I thought you left already." Laura, the resident cook, asked when she greeted her.

"This girl had fun in the forest." She answered with a chuckle.

The old woman glanced at her.

"I can see that."

Mira laughed some more. She removed the leaves and twigs from the skirt she was wearing. The pair of muddy boots that she had on has a lot to say regarding her adventure in the forest.

"I can hear your stomach, girly."

The petite woman sent a grateful smile towards the cook when she placed a plate of food in front of her. Her stomach growled some more when she perceived the delicious aroma of the grilled steak. There was a portion of boiled potatoes and stir fry carrot and peas inside the plate. Laura placed a glass of water beside the plate.

"Eat up, Mira. I have muffins if you want them."

"Thank you, Laura. You're a lifesaver."

"I know. This pack would starve without me." With another grateful smile sent towards the woman, Mira started her dinner while Laura continued cleaning the kitchen.

"Where's Alpha Lander?" Mira asked.

"In his office."

"Did he eat dinner yet?"

"Almost every one already did. The alpha did not have dinner with us but the luna took his food up to him."

"Really?"

"That sweet girl is good for the alpha. She always makes sure that Alpha Lander has food in his stomach." Laura uttered.

It was quite obvious that she likes the alpha's mate.

"I'm glad that his mate is settling in the pack." Mira replied sincerely.

"And she came at the right time. It is a blessing that the attacks on the pack has stopped. At least the alpha is focused on his new found mate. I thought that boy would have to wait longer."

Mira continues eating her dinner as she listens to the woman. She pours another glass of water.

"You want another portion, Mira?"

She shook her head. She might have been famished a while ago but the servings that the great cook gave her was enough for a regular werewolf and Mira was no werewolf.

"A muffin, perhaps?" Mira burped.

She covered her mouth in embarrassment. However, Laura looked at her with gentleness.

"The food is great, Laura. You're a goddess."

The old woman gave her a knowing smile.

"That's what they always say when they have their stomachs full."

"Because it's the truth."

"Don't bother about those dishes, Mira. This old goddess can still wash plates."

Laura said when Mira was about to go wash her plate. She placed them back on the table and pushed toward the other woman. "Wash up, girly. Remove that mud off your face."

She beamed at the older woman.

"Goodnight, Laura."

"Goodnight."

Mira replied before walking towards the Alpha's quarter. The adventure she had that day was already taking a toll on her. If only she could use her ability to teleport, she would not be this tired. Well, she has not perfected that ability yet. One time, instead of arriving to the intended place she landed in another place. But at least it was not another State or country unlike the first time. Besides, she did not want the people of the pack to have any uncertainty towards her. She did not tell the Alpha of who she is. Lander thought that she is human, a regular human. She did not see the need for them to know that she is in fact a witch. Mira was in front of her door when she come across with Liz. The tall woman was carrying a tray with empty dishes on top. She must be from the alpha's suite.

"Hello, Mira. I haven't see you in a while." Liz greeted and stopped beside her.

She nodded at the woman. "I was in the forest most of the day."

Liz looked her from head to toe. "I can tell. Dinner?"

"Done. Thank you. How's Alpha Lander?"

"Acting like a baby that he is. He acts like a joey. If only I could put him in the pocket like a koala bear." She said with a smile. Mira smiled back before looking at the tray in Liz's hand.

"I can carry the tray for you. I forgot to get water from the kitchen."

"Are you sure?"

Mira nodded. She took the tray from Liz carefully. There were two glasses and a mug on top of the plate.

"Thank you, Mira. I owe you."

"No problem."

"I should go. My little 'joey' might be looking for his momma."

They both chuckled at the woman's statement. When Liz turned around to go back to the alpha's suite, Mira did the same toward another direction. Laura was no longer in the kitchen. In fact, no one was around. A single light illuminated the area. Mira placed the tray on the counter beside the sink. She closed her eyes and inhaled deeply. She did it twice. She massaged the nape of her neck when she opened her eyes. She momentary looked at the dirty dishes before putting them in the sink. She turned on the water and washed them clean. She had to go back to the forest tomorrow. She needed more herbs for future use.

Wolf In A Sheep's Clothing

"Why is she still here in the pack?" Liz bickered.

"Because she is a good friend, darling."

"But she's human. She is not mated to anyone here in the pack."

"Liz, Mira is a huge help to the pack. The members like her. Besides, she helps in the infirmary. She was there when the attacks happened."

"Now, you're defending her, Lander. Is there anything else I need to know."

"Is my beautiful mate jealous?"

"Should I be, Lander? That woman is still around. She is gone most of the day. The medical aids said that she was not in the infirmary."

"She might be in the forest. She said she's collecting herbs for the salves she made for the injured warriors."

"Defend her some more, Lander. Is she the reason why I'm not initiated into the pack as a luna?"

"Of course not. I just want to be assured that the pack is safe. I told you before that there has been a lot of attack before you came here."

"The pack is strong already." Liz countered.

"Yes, but we can't be sure. There might be no attacks as of late but I don't want to risk the lives of the members of the pack."

"You're right. Besides, there could be a traitor spying for your every moves."

"What do you mean?" Lander questioned.

"Why don't you talk to your 'friend'? Ask her where she's at? We don't want a traitor inside the territory, right, darling?"

Mira exited the door of the Alpha. She did not bother waiting for the respond of her good friend. She was about to knock when she overheard the conversation between them. As she stayed eavesdropping, she was able to gather what she needed to know. Liz was right. Mira has been in the pack for a while. This was her longest stay in the pack. Often, she would stay for a couple of days and leave on the third day. Liz was correct when she said that she was not in the infirmary during the day. Lander was right, too, when he mentioned that she was in the forest collecting herbs.

On the eight day of her stay, Mira went to the creek. She saw a group of werewolves run past her. They must be the warriors on duty running for patrol in the territory. When she turned to the other side of the creek, there were warriors standing on guard, too. According to Lander, there was an allied agreement between Cloudless Moon pack and the neighboring pack, the La Luna. The agreement started with Lander's father, the former alpha. When Lander assumed the alpha position, he made a visit to the La Luna territory to renew the same arrangement with the alpha. Mira picked up her satchel from the rocky ground. It was almost empty. She started walking back to the pack house. With the pace that she is making, she would be in the pack house in an hour. However, she knew that it will be worth it. It was mid-afternoon when Mira left her room again. She had a short nap after her long walk from the creek.

Holding a box in hand, she marched toward the infirmary. She gave the box at the woman manning the front desk then told her that it contains the bottles of salve. After a few exchanges, Mira went out of the infirmary.

She stood outside the main entrance of the infirmary when saw a warrior sitting in the bench under an old tree. It was where she always sat. Mira shook her head and suppressed the smile that attempted to escape. She bit her lower lip then sighed before putting both of her hands inside the pockets of her cardigan. She fisted both her hands then started walking away from the infirmary. She knew that the warrior on the bench was looking at her. When the wind blew, she pulled one hand out. She opened her palm and let the powdery substance fly with them. She did it with her other hand after walking a few meters. When she arrived the pack house, her feet carried her towards the kitchen. As expected, Laura was there. She was cutting vegetables on the long island counter. She beamed at the old woman then sat opposite her.

"Have you heard the news?"

"What news?"

Laura stared at her.

"I did not see you at lunch. Are you starving yourself, girly?"

Mira shook her head. "I had a long nap. Can I have your mouth-watering muffins?"

Without a word, Laura left her. Mira placed both her elbows on top of the table. Her eyes followed Laura as the old woman got muffins from the oven. Two minutes later, Mira was munching the delicious bread. She also has a glass of milk beside the two other muffins.

"For a small woman, you sure eat a lot." Laura commented.

"You put potion in your recipe, Laura." She said with her mouth full. She drank half of the milk in one gulp. Laura filled her glass with milk again.

"Anyway, what news are you talking about?" Laura beamed at her when she grabbed another muffin.

"The alpha will be initiating his mate into the pack."

Mira stilled but continued chewing the muffin. Her appetite immediately left her. However, she finished the one she was holding to avoid offending the old woman.

"When will that be?"

"Tomorrow. Everyone is excited. Finally, this pack will have an official luna."

Laura said excitedly and continued chopping the vegetables on the table. It was quite obvious that the old woman was thrilled for the upcoming event.

"I have something for you."

The cook looked up. Her face lightened up when she saw the thing that Mira was holding. Laura lifted her hands to collect the dried flowers from her.

"It has been a while since I received flowers. My old bat of a mate preferred to give me vegetables. Ain't he sweet?" Mira chuckled. Laura inspected the dried flowers in her hand.

"Can you put those flowers in your pocket?" Mira pleaded. The old woman turned to her. Her eyes full of questions.

"Something is about to happen. I don't know what it is."

"Is this about who you are?" It was Mira's turn to stare at the old woman. Laura sent her a knowing smile.

"You knew?"

The cook shook her head.

"I don't know what you are exactly but I am sure that you're not one of us."

The petite woman exhaled.

"Just promise me that you will keep those flowers with you. They will protect you from harm. As long as I'm breathing those will keep you safe."

She gripped Laura's hand. The old woman nodded after a while.

"What's going to happen, Mira?"

"I don't know. I have a feeling in my gut that something is about to unfold."

Their serious conversation halted when two pack members entered the kitchen. Laura continued chopping the vegetables after she put the dried flowers inside her pocket. That made Mira felt better.

A Walk To Remember

"Is that Mirabella?"

Becca suppressed the grin that was about to paint her lips when she felt the jab on her stomach. She coughed in surprise then turned to face the culprit. Her beautiful mate was glaring at her. She gave her a sheepish smile instead before kissing her temple. Becca was not used to hearing her mate's full name. The tall woman also knew that her mate hates hearing it. The witch said that her full name reminded her of how old she is.

"Oh, my goddess! You don't even look a day older. I'm jealous."

A genuine smile crossed Mira's face when she faced with the former luna of the Cloudless Moon pack. They were at the entrance of the pack house. They greeted the arrival of former Alpha Lander and his mate.

"You don't look bad yourself, Rosalyn. Age suits you."

The two women embraced each other. Alpha Lander hugs his son and grandson. The mate of former Alpha Luke and the present Luna were in the kitchen to supervising the banquet. Supposedly, Becca did not want to be part of the welcoming committee but Mira insisted.

"Oh, please. Youthful look is still the trend these days." The former Luna glanced her way. "Who could this be? Your daughter?"

Becca laughs out loud. Her laughter did not stop even when Mira pinched her.

All of them were looking at the young werewolf who was laughing with no care in the world.

"If you don't stop, I swear, you're going to sleep alone." Mira threatened.

"Oh my! I'm sorry, babe." Becca apologized but the smile was still on her face. Mira stared at her angrily. Becca shut her mouth but pulled her mate towards her body.

"I'm sorry. I love you, babe." She finally said and looked at her mate with gentleness.

It seems to appease the woman.

"Behave."

Their face reddened when they found everyone looking at the both of them. Remus looked away but there is a hint of smile in his face. The older, former Alphas' both had a glint of smirk on their faces.

"So, you finally got yourself a werewolf, Mira?" It was Alpha Lander.

"Why didn't I see it?" Former Luna Rosalyn said. "You're mated and smell like us." She added after sniffing. Becca's smile widened when she found no judgment nor resentment from the older generation upon knowing that their mating consists of women.

"Well, your pack got lucky." Mira answered proudly.

"You look familiar." Alpha Lander turned to Becca. "You're a pack member, right?" She bowed a little before nodding. "I'm the daughter of Gamma Seth Jackman, Alpha Lander."

"You're that little girl who always follows Remus when he was younger."

"Yes, Luna."

"Oh? I thought you and Remus would be mates."

Instead of answering the former luna, Becca resorted to responding her with a smile.

"Lunch is ready." It was Luna Felicia.

The conversation resumed as they walked to the cafeteria. The alpha asked the help of the pack members because they would be using the cafeteria for the banquet. He also mentioned that everyone is invited for lunch. Mira was silent beside her as they made their way to the banquet. Mid-way to the dining hall Becca grabbed her mate's arm and stop walking.

"What's wrong?"

The petite woman raised her chin and stared into her eyes. There is an unnamed emotion in her baby blue eyes.

"He's the one, isn't he?" Mira said in a sad voice.

Becca met the eyes of her mate then caressed her face.

"Does it matter who he is? I have you."

Mira seemed to be looking for something in her eyes. She blinked before looking away.

"Let's get inside."

Becca stayed rooted on her feet as she followed her mate with her eyes. The cheerful start of welcoming the former alpha couple started well. The banquet has not started yet but it was already going to a different direction. She took a deep sigh. She felt a sudden heavy weight in her heart but instead of going to the banquet, she marched the opposite direction. She found herself walking towards the hill where the memories of her younger days resided. Just like she used to do, she walked under the shades of the tall trees to avoid the direct sunlight. It was the middle of the day and the heat was no joke. Nostalgia surrounded Becca when she saw the old tree where she used to sit. The tree had grown taller than she remembered. She marched toward the tree. She touched the bark like an old friend. After taking a deep sigh, she looked over the valley of cabins below. There has been quite a few number of cabins added. It expanded by a few hectares.

There was no training at this time of the day. She used to watch the warriors as they trained in the field. She even imitated their moves. It was no secret that she was fascinated by the graceful movements of the warriors and the idea of becoming her father in the future pushed to train early. To become strong and to help the pack when she gets older molded her young mind. She was very focused that training with the incoming alpha was a great idea. This hill witnessed how her and Remus' friendship started. This hill witnessed the sweat and blood she and Remus shed when they trained those years ago. This hill was the only onlooker when he and Remus agree to disagree about anything and everything under the sun. This hill shared the grief and laughter she and Remus had. This hill was the only bystander when Remus rejected her more than eight years ago.

This old tree was her only companion when she cried her heart out after the rejection. She accepted the rejection not only to save face but also for her to start her life without a mate. She remembered going home that day not just with a heavy heart but puffy eyes as well. Her father found her in the seclusion of her room. She was on the floor beside her bed and the lights were out. Gamma Seth cried with her that night. Her father helped her pack her bags. She slept in the arms of her father who held her like a fragile glass. Before the sun came up, Gamma Seth was driving her to the airport. Becca would understand if her father had held a grudge against the present alpha of the Cloudless Moon pack. He knew how much his daughter went through. Not just for the rejection but also the distance it created in their family. As far as Becca knew, no one is aware that she and Remus were mates except for her and her parents. The rejection was made private and Becca was thankful. It was not easy being the recipient of rejection. For someone who was rejected, it was a great deal. Becca knew how big of a deal it was. The struggle is far greater than anyone could ever imagine. She questioned her capability. She questioned her value. She questioned if she wanted to let someone in again, human or werewolf alike. Truth be told, Becca never indulged in any relationship, intimate or otherwise, even when she stayed in the human population for a long time. At the back of her mind, if her mate was able to let her go, why not a regular human who thought that relationship could be experimental.

She always avoided human relationship. She socialized but never accepted friendship except for Janessa. Even the young witch and her have an unconventional relationship. Their friendship started at work. Aside from the shared frustrations and common issues in the company, they never actually shared anything. Well, until Mira come along.

Oh, Mira.

Qualms

It was already nighttime when Becca entered the threshold of her parents' house. She found her parents in the kitchen having coffee.

She smiled at them and advanced to the fridge to get herself a glass of water.

"I didn't see you at the banquet." It was her mother who asked.

She poured herself a glass of milk before facing her folks. Both of them were waiting for her answer.

"I had to do something urgent."

"Mira was looking for you."

"I'll call her." She finished drinking her milk before turning her back on them. She went to the sink and cleaned the glass she had used.

"Goodnight." She kissed both their heads and walked away.

She stopped midway when her father called her name.

"My arms can accommodate you no matter how much you've grown." Becca sighed.

"I know, Dad. I love you both." She said then continued her long strides toward the comfort of her bedroom. The smell of honeysuckle invaded her senses the moment she entered the room.

She made another sigh as she closed the door. Without bothering to open the lights, she moved towards the bathroom. Becca momentarily shut Lucy out in her head. She knew that her wolf detested her at the moment but she wanted to keep her distance from everyone. She slept alone that night. That was time first since she and Mira mated. Saying it was a restless night was an understatement. Lucy keep her distance.

For the mean time, her wolf left her alone. That night before she fell asleep due to exhaustion, she and her wolf had a talk. Lucy wanted her to find their mate. However, Becca explained that she needed some time alone. At this moment, if she and Mira talk they would resort to an argument. She knew that her mate was hurt. Mira may think that she kept the identity of her first mate because she is still into him. And no matter how much explanation Becca would provide, it would just fall on deaf ears. Time and distance would be the two things that they needed at the moment.

When 5AM struck, Becca was out of her room. The lights in the kitchen were turned on, too. Her father might be awake and getting ready for the training. Not wanting another interaction with him, she ran out of the main door. After checking her shoelaces for the second time, she made a run towards the field. A good number of warriors were already there. They were doing some stretching. She made a beeline towards another direction. She followed the path to the route of the creek. Profusely sweating, she stopped when she reached the area where she and Jake had seen the vampire. Unlike the last time she was here, there were two warriors stationed in the area. On the other side, there were three more warriors from the La Luna pack. After resting for a bit, Becca began running again. This time, the course her feet took was into the hill. It was seven in the morning. Becca basked herself with the subtle heat from the sun. She found herself looking below the fields. A smile formed on her lips when she saw the warriors train. She sighed. It was just like the old days. She made herself watch the warriors as they did the exercises that were profoundly familiar.

Admittedly, she was still fascinated with the movements of the warriors. Their grace was still remarkable.

"I knew I would find you here." She almost had a whiplash when she heard that. Standing beside the tree was Alpha Remus. He was watching the training too. Becca did not know how long the alpha had been standing in the hill with her. She might have been too caught up watching over the warriors that she was not able to hear him arrive.

"Your mate looked at me differently at lunch yesterday. She knows, I presume." When she did not refute his statement, he continued.

"She's clearly bothered. She left the banquet early." Silence enveloped them. Becca had nothing to say to him. Her mind was on the woman who did not come home to her last night.

"Talk to your mate, Becca. It helps." She saw him turning his back through her peripheral vision.

"Why?" She finally had the guts to ask. It was more than eight years too late but it has been bugging her since. Alpha Remus stopped but did not turn his back.

"Because our mating was a recipe for disaster." Her eyes widened in shock. She felt really offended. She had many sleepless nights because of his rejection. She questioned her self-worth because of his rejection. She was shattered because of his rejection.

"How dare you?!" Remus faced her. His face still calm. Becca knew that her cheeks were red from fury. The anger inside her came alive. She remembered the pain she went through. She recalled the years that she had to endure being away from her family.

"A recipe for disaster, Alpha?"

When she saw that he still had that calm façade in his face, Becca did not know what came into her. She lifted her hand. She made a pushing motion towards him. She was flabbergasted when Remus was pushed five meters from where he used to stand. He lost his balance and fell on the ground. Her anger dissipated from shock. She stared at her hands.

"You have powers." Her eyes turned to Remus. He was already on his feet. It was clear from his facial expression that he was amazed with the newly found ability she had.

"Stay right there." She warned him when he was about to make a step toward her. She was glad that the alpha did what she asked him to do. Becca took in a deep sigh. She put her hands down and put them behind her back. She did not want to have a repeat of her newly found ability. She forced herself to remain calm. She looked him in the eyes. The composure was also back in his face.

"Why did you reject me?"

She heard him exhale. He stared at her. "Mother almost never made a mistake. But when I recognized that we were mates more than eight years ago, I knew in my heart that ours was an exception." He sent her a smile that solicits an understanding.

"We grew up together, Becca. I was there in your teenage years. You showed no interest towards the opposite sex. You don't even have a crush on me. An incoming alpha."

She frowned. She had no idea where his explanation was going.

"You see, I found better reaction from you when it comes to girls. I was a hormonal teenager that time but you kept me grounded. I don't know how I knew it but in my heart I knew that you were rooting for the same sex."

"W-what?"

"When I realized that you were my mate, I knew I have to let you go."

She stared at him. She stayed rooted on her feet stunned with the revelation.

"I'm sorry I hurt you, Becca. I'm sorry that I had to tell you to leave the pack territory. I had to do it or we'll be back to each other's arms. The mating bond is hard to resist. You know it by now."

Reality finally dawned on her.

Remus smirked at her.

"Looking at how you stare at Mira, I don't regret the rejection I made those years ago. That witch holds your heart in her pretty little fingers." He ended it with a chuckle.

She shook her head as a grin started showing on her face, too. She chuckled. There was nothing wrong with her. She was enough. She shook her head as those thoughts flooded her mind. Remus looked at her in amusement.

"Thank you, Alpha."

She waved at him before she made a dash from the hill.

Juana Makan

Harana

When she heard the shower stop running, Becca pulled the guitar from under the bed.

Her hands were shaking. Her heart was beating so fast. She would not be surprised if she found herself unconscious on the floor. She made an inhale-exhale motion a few times. She repeated an 'I can do this' mantra on her head. All the while, Lucy was a bystander that awaited what was going to unfold.

When she heard the knob turning, she started strumming the guitar. She was a little rusty in playing the guitar. It has been a while. She turned to music when she was in the throes of separation from her family. At least, the skills that she had acquired from that painful past came in handy. She raised her head but kept on plucking the strings. Mira came out of the bathroom. Her mate, fresh from the shower, was wearing nothing but a towel around her body. The skimpy towel showed off her sexy curves. She swallowed the lump on her throat and tried to calm herself down. She blinked her eyes to push the thoughts of jumping to the tempting distraction.

Mira stopped on her tracks when their eyes met.

There goes my heart beating

Cause you are the reason

I'm losing my sleep

Please come back now

Her mate looked away. That did not deter her. She carried on singing her heart out.

And there goes my mind racing

And you are the reason
That's why I'm still breathing
I'm hopeless now

I'd climb every mountain
And swim every ocean
Just to be with you
And fix what I've broken
Oh, 'cause I need you to se1e
That you are the reason

There goes my hand shaking
And you are the reason
My heart keeps bleeding
I need you now

A smile formed in her lips when she saw Mira bite her lower lip. Despite not looking her way, Becca continue on serenading her mate. The little reaction she got from the petite woman fueled her heart.

If I could turn back the clock
I'd make sure the light defeated the dark
I'd spend every hour of every day
Keeping you safe
I'd climb every mountain

And swim every ocean
Just to be with you—

Her singing stopped when Mira flung herself towards her. Becca let go of the guitar immediately and surrounded her arms at the petite body of her woman. She sniffed the vanilla scented hair of the woman in her arms. She let go of her when Mira pushed her then grinned when her mate removed the guitar between them. Mira got rid of the straps from her shoulder with urgency. With the hindrance between finally gone, her witch mate pulled her again. She walked backward until the back of her knees touched the side of the bed. She chuckled when they fell on top of it.

"Are we good?"

Mira looked down since it was the tall woman who was lying on her back. A hint of smile was forming at the older woman's lips. They stared at each other as if memorizing each and every freckle in their faces.

"I love you."

Mira kissed her like she always did instead of saying the words back. Becca kissed her back but end the kiss a minute sooner. The petite woman was frowning when their lips parted. However, her fingers were playing with the hairs in her nape. She caressed Mira's face. She smirked when her mate leaned on her palm.

"We need to talk."

"Is this the part where you're going to ask for space?"

"Babe, a night away from each other's arms is enough."

"Break up like what kids these days do?" Becca shook her head. She understood the sadness that surrounded the woman in her arms. She strokes Mira's back with her other hand. She felt her shiver.

"Remus and I had a talk."

The petite woman stilled on top of her before looking away. She was about to move away when Becca put both her arms around her back. A lone tear drops from her mate's face. More followed.

"Babe, you're wasting those tears for no reason." She said. She wanted to wipe those tears away but she was afraid that if she removed her arms from where they were at the moment, her mate would leave. She ain't called mushroom by her brother for nothing.

"I love you."

Mira pressed her face on her shoulder. Her cries turned to sobs.

"I love you." She repeated.

Despite the wetness pooling up on Becca's shirt, Mira continued her cries. She kissed her almost dry hair. Becca shifted their position. She was now hovering on top of her mate. Tears were still flowing from her close eyes. She kissed both eyes and her button nose. She pressed light kisses on top of the freckles in her cheeks and the bridge of her nose. Her kisses made a path towards her neck. Mira made a room so she could kiss her better.

"I love you." She whispered before leaving wet kisses at the back of her ear. Her ministrations continued towards the scattered freckles on her shoulder. She found them appealing that she had to pay more attention to each and every freckle. As her mouth made a trail of kisses, her hand was making its own course below. Her mate moaned when her hand reached its final target. She raised her head to look at her mate. She was in the valley of her well endowed front. She watched how her wet lashes flutter when she made a move with her finger. Mira's mouth went ajar when she did it again. Her eyes opened widely when Becca inserted two fingers inside her without preamble. Mira finally met her eyes.

"I love you." She pulled her fingers out before pushing it back in again. Mira bit her lower lip to hold back the sounds of pleasure from leaving her mouth. Becca continued her thrust until Mira pulled her head in for a searing kiss. When she felt her entrance gripping her fingers, she stopped. She lifted her face from hers. Mira was pulling her back but she refused to kiss her again.

"Please." The petite woman cried.

Her voice was a little raspy. Might be from crying or at what was taking place at the moment.

"I love you." Becca whispered.

"Babe, please." Mira thrust her lower body towards her but Becca refused to budge.

"I love you."

"Becca, please."

"I love you."

Her mate grabbed both her shoulders. Her beautiful blue eyes were blazing with annoyance.

"I love you, goddamit! Kiss me now!"

"I love you, too, babe."

She met her mate's lips half way as her hand continued its work. Becca smiled as they kissed while Mira's grip on her shoulder tightened. Her mate bit her lower lip when she reached her peak. The tall woman embraced her mate as she waited for her to descend from her high. Mira released a contented sigh. She pecked her lips twice before laying beside her. She covered her with the bath towel she had on a while ago.

"I love you, babe." She whispered as she spooned her. Mira huffed but did not say another word. However, she did not protest when Becca pulled her closer.

"I love you."

She pressed butterfly kisses at the back of the petite woman's ear. She told her again that she loves her. She said it on repeat.

"I love you, too." Mira replied.

Becca chuckled. Finally.

Lucy's Day Out

Becca smiled when she felt the tight hold of her mate on her mane.

Lucy was currently having the time of her life. She was in her wolf form and Mira was riding on her back. They were running in the forest. Mira was giving her the directions. Apparently, they have to gather herbs. And these herbs were located at the heart of the forest. She stopped when her mate told her to stop, She lowered herself on the forest floor. Mira gets down from her back.

Lucy showered her face with kisses when they faced each other. Her beautiful mate chuckled at her wolf's antics.

"Have fun while I get the plants I need." Mira kissed her snout before turning her back. Lucy barked twice before running. She sprinted over the fallen logs. When she was a few meters away from their mate, she glanced at Mira's direction. The petite woman is already inspecting a certain plant. She saw her smelling the leaf. Lucy scrunched her nose. Her head turned to her left when she heard a sound. She galloped when she saw the squirrel. They circled the area until the squirrel climbed a tree. Lucy growled in annoyance. Becca was laughing at her wolf. Lucy resorted to a whimper but the terrified animal refused to return to the ground. The annoyed wolf scratched the bark of the tree to no avail. The squirrel remained on the thick branch.

"Let the poor animal go."

"I want to play."

"But the animal thought you would eat him."

"That's possible, too."

'Stop it. Where's our mate?"

Lucy glanced around. Her wolf whined when she did not see Mira. She did not notice that she already ran a great distance from where her mate was. She sniffed then headed to the direction of the strong scent of honeysuckle. Lucy grinned when she saw their mate having fun in the middle of the field. Tongue lolling on the side, she lay on her stomach as she watched the blue-eyed woman. Her attention was distracted when a small butterfly landed on her nose. Lucy stilled. Her eyes widened when both of its wings swayed. She whined when the butterfly flew away. However, she made happy barks when more butterflies of different colors and sizes surrounded her. They were flying above her, circling her head. She tried to catch one of them but it flew faster than she could jump.

"You like that, Lucy?"

Her wolf took a quick look at their mate before barking at the butterflies. Mira chuckled at the werewolf. When Lucy got tired of chasing the colorful insect she laid on the ground. She put her paws on the air and scratched her back on the grassy floor. She kept her paws suspended on the air and moved it like walking on air. After a few minutes she picks up the backpack from where Mira had put them. She carried them to the back of the big tree. A couple of minutes later, Becca came out. She had on a black racer back top and a black track shorts. She sat between the wide roots of a big tree then placed the bag beside her.

Mira was still busy collecting the plants only she knows and for whatever purposes it maybe. She laid her head on the big tree then closed her eyes. The serenity of the place lulled her into a sleepy mode. She only had a few hours of sleep the previous night. Grin painted her lips. She and Mira had had a long night. They made love until their limbs could not take it anymore. So far, the make up sex had been great. The shorter period of sleep has been worth it.

"What's on your mind, wolfie?"

Becca opened her eyes. Mira was looking down at her. The large satchel she has on her hand was almost half full.

"You in my bed naked and sated." Blush was immediate at her mate's cheeks. She laughed out loud.

"Get your mind out off the gutter." Her mate threw the satchel on her. Still laughing, she closed the lid before putting it inside the back pack beside her.

"Are we done here?" Mira nodded.

The tall woman stood up. She pulled her mate towards her body and embraced her tight. Mira put her arms around her back and leaned on her chest.

"I love you, babe."

"I love you, too."

"It ain't so bad, right?"

"Stop ruining the moment, babe." She kissed her head before letting go.

"I should shift. Lucy is whining so loud that my ears are ringing." Mira laughed at her.

"Go. It's Lucy's time with me." A peck on the lips later, Lucy was back with Mira. Like always, the wolf showered her mate with kisses. More wet kisses later, Lucy got down on her belly so that Mira could ride on her back. When their mate already made herself comfortable, Lucy stood up. Mira embraced her arms on Lucy's neck. They made their way back. They passed the warriors on duty. Some were on their wolf forms. Mira held her thigh firmly on Lucy's both sides when the wolf ran faster. The grip she had on the wolf's neck tightened. Before long, they stopped in front of the Jackman's cabin. Mira slide on Lucy's side. She faced the wolf. One of her hands was combing the soft and fluffy fur on her neck.

"I had fun, Lucy."

The wolf gave their mate kisses, slobbers and all. Mira closed her eyes with a smile. She closed both her arms around the wolf. Her fingers were threading on the soft fur.

"I love you, Lucy. I love you and your human."

Mira opened the main door of the house. She already knew where the keys were hidden. Lucy ran inside before Mira could even make a step into the threshold. With a smile, Mira flicked her hand twice. She knew that the wolf would scurry towards the bedroom then bathroom. Becca already told her that her wolf was addicted to baths. Very particularly with shampoos and its scents too. When Mira entered their room, she already heard the sound of shower and splashing of water. Happy barks echoed in the bathroom. With a smile she put the back pack down. She prepared clothes for Becca then searched for the new sets of towels. She hung it at the door knob. She removed the cardigan she was wearing. The shoes, socks and the pants followed. Lucy would take so much time inside the shower judging from the sound Lucy was creating. Becca would have so much cleaning to do after her wolf's bath. She laid on the bed. The bed was tempting her exhausted body. She stretched like a cat then grabbed the pillow on Becca's side of the bed. The smell of her mate lingered on it. She hugged the pillow. Less than two minutes, she was out like a light.

Calm Before The Storm

Becca immediately opened her eyes when her hand touched an empty space. She looked around the room but did not see her mate. There was no sound coming from the bathroom too. She got down from the bed. She grabbed her jacket from the hook at the back of the door before leaving the room. She went to the kitchen and made two mugs of coffee. She already saw Mira's form in the patio. Holding the tray in hand, Becca made her way to her mate. She placed the hot drink on top of the table. Mira beamed at her when she saw the coffee. She untied the jacket on her waist then placed it on her mate's shoulder before sitting on the chair beside the petite woman. This was not the first time that she woke up in bed without Mira by her side. It was the third since they came back to the territory her mate has been experiencing restless night. Often, Mira would jolt awake in her arms. She learned from her mate that someone was trying to take down the barrier. Since the barrier around the territory is connected with Mira, every time someone was attempting to remove the protection using black magic, she felt it.

"Where is it this time?"

"South." Mira answered before sipping the coffee.

"The attempt is stronger this time."

"You didn't go there, right?" Her mate shook her head.

"You won't go anywhere without me. Right, babe?"

"I won't. Not without you."

Becca smiled at the confirmation.

"Come here. I miss your warmth. You left me alone. You know that I hate it when you do that."

Mira grabbed her outstretched hand before transferring onto her lap. The petite woman made herself comfortable in her arms as they drank their coffee. They were in the middle of a conversation when Mira suddenly jerked. Becca immediately give her mate a once over. She caressed Mira's face.

"Where?"

"In the creek."

"How are you?"

"Still okay. Good thing we are not having sex at the moment."

The tall woman laughed. Her mate still had her sense of humor despite the circumstance. When the gamma went out for the training, the mated couple decided to get ready for the day. Becca was with her mother when she received a call from her mate. A couple of hours ago, she sent Mira to the alpha's office after her father mind linked her that the alpha needed the witch for an urgent matter. Mira was waiting for her in front of the pack house. She was with the alpha and former alpha Lander. She bowed at the alphas before smiling at her blue-eyed mate. She kissed her temple.

"Shall we?" Frowning, she turned to her mate when she heard that from Alpha Remus.

"We are going to the creek. We are meeting the alpha of La Luna pack." Becca nodded. Alpha Remus changed into his massive Black wolf followed by Alpha Lander's Dark Brown.

"Go, babe. I'm riding you." Mira said with a smile

Lucy started yapping in her head. She grinned at her mate before changing into her wolf. When Mira settled on her back, the two alpha wolfs started running to the direction of the creek. Lucy barked happily as she followed them.

Mira embraced her neck tightly as they ran. Becca felt stronger. In every sprint she made, she felt physically powerful. She has been feeling like that since they came back to the territory. Becca wondered if it had to do with the recent mating of hers and Mira. Lucy informed her that she felt the same whenever she runs as a wolf. After few minutes of running, they stopped few meters from the bank. There were at least five warriors there and double in numbers on the other side. The two alpha's walked behind a tree so that they could return to their human counterpart. The members of the pack often hid sets of clothes under the trees for emergency cases.

"Baby, I want Becca back."

Lucy was about to go when Mira pulled the mane on her neck. The wolf whined. The petite woman beamed at her mate.

"Stay. Change back into Becca."

The wolf barked while staring at the witch. She barked again a few more times. She moved her neck to remove Mira's hand. Her mate laughed at her. The blue eyed woman pulled the wolf's head so they could look each other in the eye.

"Change into Becca. Trust me." She kissed the wolf's snout when it whined again.

"Please. I love you."

Lucy whined again but she obeyed woman who held her heart. A few seconds later, Becca was standing two feet beside her. Mira was grinning widely as she looked at her. On the other hand, the tall woman was minding her appearance. Wide-eyed, Becca looked at herself in bewilderment. She and Lucy was making a fuse a while ago before transforming into human. They both knew that once a wolf transformed into her human counterpart, the human would be stark naked. Still confused, Becca turned to her beaming mate. A Playful smile still plastered on her woman's face.

"I told you to trust me, babe. I wouldn't let these wolves catch a sight of what's mine."

Chuckling, Becca pulled her mate. She gave Mira a peck on the lips.

"I love you, too."

"That was awesome, Mira. You should have told me that you could do that. This old man don't need to walk that far to have his clothes on." Alpha Lander said as he paced towards them.

"It was still on experimental stage. Besides, my woman need not to show her body to anyone else." The old alpha laughed at the witch. Remus was smiling at them. Becca squeezed her mate's palm when she saw the petite woman glare at the current alpha. She put her arm around Mira and pulled her closer.

She kissed her temple and whisper how much she loves her.

The shifter smiled when Mira placed her arms on her back before saying the words back.

"The witch has a sweet bone."

"Shut up, Lander."

Becca chuckled together with the former alpha. She suddenly bit her lower lip when she felt the pinch on her side.

"They are here."

They glanced at the other side of the creek. Asides from the warriors from a while ago, two other men stood at the bank. They were looking back at them.

Alpha Lander nodded at Mira. Becca hold on to her mate as the petite woman touched the shoulder of the former alpha.

Not a second later, they were on the other side. The alpha of the La Luna pack together with his entourage was surprised when they appeared two meters away from where they stood.

"Alpha H." Remus greeted.

The taller, buffer guy nodded at him. They shook each other's hand before they turned to the rest of Remus' backup.

"This is my grandfather, former alpha Lander. This is Mira and Becca."

"Nice to meet all of you. This is also my beta, Moragg."

"Where did you find the bodies?" Alpha Lander asked.

"Follow me." The Alpha turned his back and marched toward the trees. The smell of blood assaulted their nose when they set their foot under the first tree.

"The first body was found here." Alpha H pointed at the splattered blood on the grass. "The second one was under that tree and third one was three meters away."

Their eyes followed the direction that the alpha was pointing.

"The bodies were already cold when they were found by the patrol at 6AM."

"The killing happened at 3Am. I felt them trying to enter the territory." Mira disclosed.

"I'm sorry for your loss, Alpha."

"Who are these people?"

"It is an old acquaintance. A vampire."

The two members of the La Luna pack turned to the older Alpha in surprise.

"How are we going to protect ourselves from these bloodsuckers? I thought our kind is in good relationship with them." The beta said. Clearly, he is baffled by the news.

"It's true, Beta Moragg, but this one is out for revenge."

"Why?"

"I killed his mate."

Alpha H and Beta Moragg turned to Mira.

"He wanted to claim the Cloudless Moon pack's territory so he used his mate to seduced Lander."

"His mate claimed to be my mate but Mira saved me from my doom. They used a potion to make me believe them." Alpha Lander added.

"That's fucked up."

"To sum it up, son."

"What are we going to do?"

"My niece is coming later. She will protect your territory like I did with theirs. The next blood that will shed will be his."

"You're a witch?"

"Yes, Alpha."

"And I'm her bodyguard."

The four of the male werewolves turned to Becca. She put her hands up and made a peace sign. Eventually, Alpha Remus and former alpha Lander returned to the Cloudless Moon territory. Mira and Becca were left behind to prepare La Luna for the pending confrontation with the vampires.

The Clash

Mira nodded when Becca glanced at her. With a sigh, the tall woman mind linked her father to tell him that it was time. Earlier that afternoon, Alpha Remus had sent the children and those who could not fight to a safe area. Mira placed a spell around the area for precautionary measures. Becca stood beside her mate then pulled the witch to her body. Mira encircled both her arms on her back. The shifter lifted her mate's chin so that she could look at her baby blues. Determination plastered on the witch' face.

"We are going on a very long vacation after this."

The older woman grinned.

"I like that."

"Babe, please be safe."

"I promise. Just don't do anything stupid."

"I promise. I love you."

"And I love you."

Their lips met halfway. As their kiss deepened Mira put her hand around Becca's nape. They separated when someone cleared his throat. Becca pecked Mira's lips before hugging her again. She chuckled when her mate glared at Remus who was already beside them.

"We're leaving the territory when we're done here." The petite woman said to her before moving out of her arms.

"Yes, ma'am."

When they reached the bank near the creek, Becca stood beside the other warriors as planned. Alpha Remus and Mira stood out front. The warriors of the La Luna pack were facing them on the other side. The alpha and the beta were standing in front of the warriors too. Becca saw Janessa behind alpha H. Even from afar it was visible that the young boss was frowning. She knew perfectly why. Mira stood straight. Becca suddenly felt nervous. The anxiety she felt multiplied. A surge of wind passed, If not for the enhanced hearing of the werewolves they would not have noticed. They were not surprised when they saw several men and women standing five meters away from them. It was the same on the other side of the creek.

"You're good."

They looked at the man leading the vampires. It was the same man she and Jake saw a few days ago.

"I got your message. I don't want to disappoint that's why I prepared a welcoming committee."

"Mirabella. The ever reliant Mirabella." He said like a lover.

"I'm flattered. Thanks, Rudolf."

The vampire chuckled. He looked around like he was inspecting the expanse of his property.

"By the way, tell you minions to stop poking. It tickles."

Mira and the vampire stared at each other. The smirk still stayed on the vampire leader's. Suddenly a vampire from the back sprinted towards them. The warriors growled. However, the said vampire flew back when he was about three meters away from where Mira and Alpha Remus stood. The vampire was propelled to an invisible wall. The place he bumped into sizzled like an electric current. Rudolf gritted his teeth in annoyance. More vampires jumped simultaneously into the invisible wall. The same thing happened. Every place they touched sizzled.

"You want to try them yourself, Rudolf?" Rudolf turned to Mira. Composure was back on his face. He smiled at the witch as he put his right hand in the air like was about to swear an oath. Several vampires on the other side of the creek ran towards the La Luna territory. They suffered the same fate. Rudolf clapped his hands. He shakes his head as he stares at Mira.

"Amazing. You're a remarkable witch."

"Thank you."

"But you have to die. I came prepared, too."

A surge of wind came. It stopped when two men stood besides Rudolf. One a vampire and another a werewolf. Another vampire stood at the other side of the shifter. Gasps and growls emitted from the Cloudless Moon pack. Mira swallowed but stayed calm as she glanced at the werewolf the vampires chose to take as a hostage. The abducted werewolf stared at the witch. The words were muffled due to the gag in his mouth. In any other circumstance, Mira would have made fun of him at the current state he was in.

"Did I strike a nerve, Mirabella?"

The witch shrugged. However, the werewolves kept on growling knowing that one of them was in danger. A scream echoed in the night. It was heard again when Rudolf smashed his hand at the werewolf torso for the second time. Mira sighed before she asked.

"What do you want?"

"A mate for a mate."

The werewolf shook his head furiously. Mira stared at the vampire. Her face still emotionless. Her left hand was on the small of her back. The knuckle was firmly close.

"I know who your mate is, Mira. Right, pup?" He removed the gag from the werewolf who starts kicking despite the strong grip on both his arms.

"NO! Don't let him get my sister!"

The strong façade that Mira put up crumbled when she felt the hand that grasped her forearm. Its warmth utterly familiar.

"No." She replied without looking at the woman beside her.

"It's okay, babe."

"No."

Becca turned her body so that they could look at each other. Fear evident on the witch's face as she met her mate's eyes. The tall woman held Mira's face. She smiled at her mate.

"I trust you. I want you to trust me, too." Mira shook her head.

"Please."

Becca pulled her mate in for an embrace. The petite woman held her tighter.

"Touche'." The shifter hugged her mate closer to her body then kissed her temple.

"Let's kill this son of a bitch, babe." She whispered. She glanced at the alpha and nodded at him. Remus remained impassive.

"I love you." A peck on the lips, Becca let go of her mate. She walked forward until she was two meters away from Rudolf and her brother.

"Let my brother go."

"Becky, no."

"It's fine, baby boy."

"How sweet." Rudolf said and motioned on the vampires to let go of the young male werewolf. Pain and regret showed on Jake's as he gazed at his sister. He walked forward when one vampire pushed him. Becca took in a sigh of relief when Jake walked past her. She raised her head and stared into the eyes of the vampire who had caused pandemonium in her home. Rudolf grinned at her. She smirked back.

"Now, babe." She screamed before moving both her hand forward. Confusion struck on both sides as Rudolf and two of his underlings flew back. They fell on the shallow waters of the creek. Becca did not bother to glance at her mate. She knew that not one vampire could ever come near her. They flew away when they come as close as two meters. The shifter kept her focus on every vampire her eyes caught on. Her hands keep on moving. When she saw a vampire collide on the invisible wall and sizzle like an electrocuted animal, she kept on sending every blood sucker there. When Becca took time to breath, she heard the growling of the warriors. She noticed that not one from both pack had changed into their wolf. They seemed to be astounded with what they had witnessed. Most of the shifters she saw were wide-eyed. Becca also realized that she stood at the place outside the barrier Mira had made. She became aware that Mira and Janessa were standing near the banks on both sides. The tall woman jolted from her daze when Rudolf plummeted on her side. The vampire was screaming but no sound was heard. His hands were on his back but it was fastened by an unseen tie.

"The decision is yours, Alpha."

Remus nodded. He looked ahead. Alpha H was awaiting his decision too. In a split second, Janessa was beside them with Alpha H in tow. The alpha of the La Luna was disoriented too. Becca knew the feeling a little too well.

"Alpha H, what's your verdict?"

"Death."

Alpha Remus nodded in agreement. He glanced at Mira. The witch clicked her thumb and index finger. They separated altogether when Rudolf burst into flame. The minions who followed him were enveloped in fire too.

"I'm so ready for a vacation." Becca stated with joy. She even put her one hand up.

"Oh, no. Your reliever ain't good enough to do your job." Janessa exclaimed in protest.

"Whatever you say." Becca pulled her mate and kissed her on the mouth with vigor. She heard Janessa huff in protest.

"I love you." It was Mira who uttered the words first when their kiss ended.

"I love you, too." She said back, grinning.

Slumber Party

Despite the exhausting day, the members of the Cloudless Moon pack were high spirited. There was no blood spilled from the side of the neighboring packs. The warriors went back to their post while others went home. Mira did not remove the warding spell around the pack. Even though the cause of the problem was already gone, the witch did not want risk the safety of the pack. She still thought of the possibility of Rudolf having a plan B. The main door of the Jackman's cabin was open when they reached home. Olive was waiting outside together with Gamma Seth. They must have been informed that everything will be alright. That they already won.

The moment they stepped their feet into the pack ground, the pack doctor reached for her injured son. After a quick glance at his son, the gamma turned to his first born. Without another word, he pulled the couple in his arms. He kissed their heads simultaneously.

"I'm fine, dad. We are fine."

"I know. My wolf needs assurance that his pups are alright."

When gamma Seth let them go, Olive and Jake were nowhere in sight.

"Are you okay, Mira?"

The witch smiled. "Yes. Thank you, Seth."

"No, Mira. Thank you. Without you, more lives could have been lost tonight."

"Piece of cake." The petite woman said as she shrugged.

The father and daughter laughed at her. They found Olive and Jake in the kitchen. The pack doctor was done giving first aid to the youngest Jackman. Jake was holding a bag of frozen peas on his face. Becca sat beside her brother in the dining table. Jake placed the peas down before glancing at her. His right brows had lacerations. His left jaw up to his cheek was discolored. His lower lip was busted. It was also noticeable that his knuckles were bruised.

"What happened, Jake?"

"I was going home from downtown. They ambushed the car I was driving."

"Do you want to go to the infirmary?" It was Seth. He sat at the head of the table.

"I'll be fine, dad. I just need to sleep this off." Becca looked up when she saw her mate at the back of Jake's chair. The petite woman smiled.

"Can I, Jakey?" Her brother did not bother to turn. He nodded. Mira placed her left palm on top of Jake's head. Becca's eyes widened when she saw a foggy blur coming from her palm towards her brother's head. Jake looks sleepy while this was happening. Her mate's palm moved towards his face. Becca's mouth went ajar when she saw the damage in his face slowly disappear in front of her very eyes. If not for her fast reflexes Mira would have sprawled on the ground. She picked up her mate and carried her into the living room. Full of worry, she laid her down on the couch. Her breath was shallow and her eyes were closed.

"Mom!"

"Is she pregnant, Becky?" It was Jake who followed them.

"Shut up! Mom!"

"What happened? Give her a room."

The two men immediately made space for Olive. She knelt beside Becca before grabbing Mira's hand and checking for her pulse. Her hand stayed on her wrist as she stared at the watch in her wrist. Before Becca could utter another word, Mira opened her eyes.

"Babe? Oh, babe." The tall woman caressed her mate's face. Her face laced with concern.

"How do you feel? You scared me."

"Are you pregnant, fossil?" Jake blurted.

"Are you okay, Jakey?"

"Yes. Thank you. Are you alright?"

Becca helped her mate to sit properly. She sat beside her and pulled her to her side then kissed her temple.

"What happened, babe?"

"Drink this." It was Olive holding a glass of water.

"If you're feeling better, were having pizza. It's on the table." She said with a smile. Becca assisted her mate as she drank from the glass. Her dad and Jake followed her mom to the kitchen.

"I'm hungry, babe." Mira muttered.

"What happened?"

"Too much magic requires too much energy." The shifter pulls her mate into her lap. She embraces her tighter. Mira take in a deep sigh as she leans on her.

"You had me worried, babe."

"I'm sorry."

"I love you."

"I love you, too. Can we have that pizza now? I'm really hungry." The tall woman chuckled. Hand in hand, they went to the kitchen. Her family were already munching on the pizza. She guided Mira to a chair before getting them plates and glasses. Becca was on her second slice when she saw the time. She smiled to herself. It was 3 o'clock in the morning and yet they were in the kitchen having pizza. The two male Jackman smiled also. They must have noticed the time too since they glanced at the clock on the wall.

"What are your plans, Becky?" Beta Seth asked. She turned to her father.

"We're leaving later after lunch."

"Alpha Remus would let you stay."

"I know, mom, but I'm more comfortable with Mira outside the pack." She glanced at her mate. "I want to give my mate a peace of mind that she's the only one regardless who came first." Her smile widened when she noticed the redness of her mate's face. She grabs Mira's hand and kisses the back of her palm.

"You and Remus already have a mate of your own, Becky. You can stay. Mira will always be welcome in the pack."

"I know, mom."

"What do you mean?" It was Jake. He was frowning. All of them looked at the youngest person in the group. He had stopped eating and he was scowling at them.

"Alpha Remus has to do with Becky not living with us?"

"It was a long time ago, Jake. I moved on. I found my second chance in Mira."

Mira beamed back at her before squeezing the hand that was intertwined with hers.

"He rejected you?" Jake asked, flabbergasted. "Why? How could he do that?"

"Because he wants the best for me." She answered her brother. She turned to her mate and stared into her baby blues.

"He knew that he was not the right person for me. That the moon goddess made a mistake by pairing us together."

"What?" The three Jackmans said together.

She smiles as she glances at them. Her eyes returned to the beautiful woman beside her. Mira has glassy eyes as she stared at the shifter.

"Mira Doue, thank you for giving me a chance to be with you. Thank you for not giving up on this bond." Her mate caressed her face with her other hand.

"I've waited for a long time for you. Why should I give you up? If you think you're not enough, I'm more than enough for the two of us."

Becca chuckled before kissing the palm of her hand.

"I love you, old woman." The tall woman shifted before her mate could utter a response. She knelt beside Mira's chair. Still holding Mira's hand, she pulled out the ring from her pocket. She rubbed the ring with her fingers when she saw it was tangled with the dried heathers. She blew on it to remove the dust on top of the peacock shade sapphire ring she had bought. She stared at her mate's blue eyes. She was right. The ring compliments her eyes.

"Miss Doue, it is an honor to share my life with you. Will you marry me?"

Regardless of the giddy reaction from her mother, her eyes remained on her mate. Mira pouted as tears fell on her cheeks. The petite woman put her arms around her neck. She stood up. Her mate still in her arms. She heard the soft sobbing from the woman in her arms.

"I love you, Becca." The witch said in muffled voice.

"Is that a yes?" She pulls her mate a little when she felt her nod. She cupped her face between her hands.

"I will marry you, wolfie."

She heard her father and brother whistle when Mira expressed the confirmation of their engagement. With a laugh, she pushed the ring into her finger before kissing her on the lips. She hugs her mate again.

"I love you, babe."

The Happiest Hello

Grinning, Becca focused her attention back to the files sent by the account officers. The quarterly meeting was scheduled on Friday. She still had three days to work on the documents she had received. She already reviewed the file organized by the temporary reliever that she trained before she left. The reliever did a great job but Janessa being the perfectionist said it was not good enough. The young boss insisted that Becca should return to her post.

Two hours later, the account manager stood from her chair. Her job was half done. She still needed the files from the major accounts. A cup in hand, she returned to the sanctuary of her office. A smile formed on her lips when her eyes stumbled on the wooden vase beside the monitor of the desktop computer. The wooden vase has several dried heathers on it. Without realizing it, she sniffed. Sweet scent assaulted her nose. She shook her head. Mira had put a fresh batch of dried heather in her office yesterday. Suffice it to say, her mate sprayed her voodoo potion on the heather. Beaming at the flowers, she sat in her chair. Between the both of them, Mira was more possessive. She never admitted that she was jealous but she threatened Becca every time she did. However, the tall woman just laughs it off. She loves it when Mira exercise her right to be a green-eyed witch. She loves it when her mate was being possessive. Becca loves what follows after the threats. Surely, she paid for the jealousy acts. She became the recipient of pinching and all but the make-up sex was great. Mira was very thorough and attentive. It was worth it. Becca shakes her head. Her mind was clouded with sensual thoughts. She drank her coffee and went back to working mode. She was in the middle of analyzing the sales report from the supervisor of a known mall when she felt a kiss in her cheek. It was followed by an embrace on her shoulders. Smiling widely, she glanced at the beautiful woman who owned the most striking blue eyes but was a green-eyed monster when she feels like it.

"Hi." Mira beamed at her. Her mate stood up and turned the swivel chair she was sitting on.

"Hello there, wife. I miss you."

"I miss you, too." Becca pulled her mate. Mira leaned on her front. She put her hands around the petite woman as they shared a long, passionate kiss. Another peck on the lips, Mira sat on her laps. Becca placed her hands around her middle. She sniffed her neck.

"What have you been doing?" She whispered.

"I cleaned the house. It was a little messy." She laughs. Unpacked boxes were in her living room when she left the apartment in the morning.

"I told you to wait for me, babe."

"It's fine."

"Did you use your voodoo magic?"

"If I remember it right, you also share some of my voodoo magic."

Becca chuckled. "Yes, I do. I love you, witchy babe."

"Shut up." They already talked about the gifts that Becca acquired. Mira said that it must have been due to them being mated. However, the telekinesis was the only thing that Becca obtained from her mate. The shifter even joked that she should start reading potion books. Instead of reprimanding her, Mira told her to start studying the basic. Supportive, eh.

"Have you told Janessa that your name plate needs changing?"

"Not yet. I was a little preoccupied since we returned. Maybe later?"

Instead of answering her, Mira put her hand out. She made a few hand gestures. Becca watched the name plate hanging on the door moved in the air. When it stopped moving, it faces them.

"That's more like it." Her mate said followed by a satisfied sigh.

BECCA DOUE-JACKMAN
Account Manager

"I like it, too." She kissed her temple and held her hand. She grinned when her finger grazed the accessory on Mira's finger. She grabs it and stares at the two jewelries. One of them matched with hers. She kissed her hand before intertwining them with hers. She and Mira got married a month after they left the Cloudless Moon Pack. The wedding was made private with family only. It was a mutual decision. After the wedding, the couple flew to Croatia. Apparently, Mira has not been to the said country in decades. They stayed there for two weeks that the petite woman was able to gain tan line. Becca kissed the freckles on her wife's shoulder.

"I should go to Janessa. Finish your job. We need to be home early." Her mate stood up but Becca refused to let go of her hand.

"Are you going to stay in her office?"

"Yes. I will be waiting for you there."

"Alright. Give me two hours."

Mira nodded. She kissed her before leaving her alone in the office. Becca watched her mate as she went out of the office. Her eyes caught a glimpse of the name plate on the door. She smiled before turning her chair back to the reports awaiting her undivided attention. However, the photo frame on the left side of the monitor, near the Bluetooth mouse caught her eyes. It was the picture of her and Mira. Her mate had her arms around her shoulders from the back. The hands that showed off their rings were side by side. They were smiling in the picture. Happiness reflected in their eyes. The photo was taken during their wedding reception. They both love the picture. They even have a bigger one at home. It was Mira's idea to have the photo in her office.

She said it would clearly show everyone who owned her. Becca just laughed it off. Personally, she was very proud to show off that she is married and mated to Mirabella Doue. Being mated to her granted her happiness. Mira is a blessing. She represents the second chance at happiness that the moon goddess provided her with. All those years ago that she suffered from rejection, having Mira has been worth it. She knew that there would be more bumps in their journey but having her mate beside her would surpass it all. When the monitor of the computer turned off, Becca stood up. She grabs the messenger bag and locks the door of the office. She climbs the stairs toward the office of the marketing director. Ruth was nowhere in sight. She knocked twice before opening the private office. Mira beamed at her when their eyes met. She grinned at her mate.

"Hello, wife. I'm ready to go home."

www.ingramcontent.com/pod-product-compliance
Lightning Source LLC
LaVergne TN
LVHW041847070526
838199LV00045BA/1485